KRISTY AND THE
SISTER WAR

**Other books by
Ann M. Martin**

Leo the Magnificat
Rachel Parker, Kindergarten Show-off
Eleven Kids, One Summer
Ma and Pa Dracula
Yours Turly, Shirley
Ten Kids, No Pets
Slam Book
Just a Summer Romance
Missing Since Monday
With You and Without You
Me and Katie (the Pest)
Stage Fright
Inside Out
Bummer Summer

THE KIDS IN MS. COLMAN'S CLASS series
BABY-SITTERS LITTLE SISTER series
THE BABY-SITTERS CLUB mysteries
THE BABY-SITTERS CLUB series
CALIFORNIA DIARIES series

THE BABY-SITTERS CLUB

KRISTY AND THE SISTER WAR

Ann M. Martin

AN
APPLE
PAPERBACK

SCHOLASTIC INC.
New York Toronto London Auckland Sydney

Cover art by Hodges Soileau

ISBN 0-590-05990-4

12 11 10 9 8 7 6 5 4 3 2 1   7 8 9/9 0 1/0

Printed in the U.S.A.   40

First Scholastic printing, October 1997

The author gratefully acknowledges
Ellen Miles
for her help in
preparing this manuscript.

CHAPTER 1

"Sit, girl, sit!"

Emily Michelle came to a halt and plopped onto her bottom. Then she grinned at me.

I cracked up. "Not you, silly," I said. "I was talking to Shannon."

"Doggie sit," said Emily Michelle.

I glanced at Shannon just in time to see her drop her hind end down obediently. She looked at Emily with an expectant tilt of her head, as if waiting for the next command. "I don't believe it!" I cried. Shannon never sits when *I* tell her to. I clapped my hands, and Shannon hopped up and pranced around. "Say it again, Emily," I said.

"Doggie sit," crowed Emily.

Shannon stopped prancing and tucked herself into a perfect sit.

I smacked my forehead and groaned. Then I picked up Emily and twirled her around. "You are an excellent dog trainer," I said, squeezing her tight. Emily squeezed me back. Shannon, eager to be part of the action, bumped up against my ankles and gave a couple of yelps.

I lowered Emily to the ground and flopped down beside her. Shannon nuzzled my ear and licked my cheek. The warm afternoon sun lit up the golden yellow leaves of the big maple tree I lay beneath, and the sky was a brilliant blue. It was a perfect fall day, a Monday in early October, and I was perfectly happy. I could think of nowhere I'd rather be, nothing I'd rather be doing. The day was made for scuffling around in the leaves with my little sister and our puppy.

I sighed with contentment. Emily and Shannon sighed too.

And now, we interrupt this perfect moment for a word from our sponsors.

Just kidding. But I should stop to explain who I am. My name's Kristy Thomas. I have brown hair and brown eyes and I'm on the short side. I'm thirteen years old and in the eighth grade at SMS (formally known as Stoneybrook Middle School). I've lived my whole life in Stoneybrook, Connecticut, and it's a pretty great place to grow up, if I do say so myself. (One thing you'll learn about me is that I'm never shy about giving my opinion.)

Emily Michelle is my sister, though you'd

never know it by looking at us. She's a little roly-poly two-and-a-half-year-old, with shiny, dark hair and shiny, dark, almond-shaped eyes. Emily Michelle was a Vietnamese orphan, but she's part of our family now. She doesn't speak much yet, but I know it won't be long before she's chattering away. I'm so glad my mom and Watson adopted her.

Who's Watson? I'll explain. But sit tight, because my family is kind of complicated, and it'll take awhile to introduce you to everyone.

First of all, there's my mom, Elizabeth Thomas Brewer, otherwise known as Superwoman. She's a true heroine, at least in my eyes. Why? Because years ago, when my father walked out on us, she didn't give up. She hung in there and raised me and my brothers (two older, one younger) on her own. And it wasn't easy, believe me. We went through some pretty hard times, but we did it together, as a family. And now things are much, much better.

See, not long ago, my mom met this sweet guy named Watson Brewer, and the two of them fell in love. (To be honest, I wasn't crazy about Watson at first — but that's changed.) And, as if love weren't enough to make my mom happy, it turned out that Watson is rich. And I mean *rich*. As in millionaire. After my mom married Watson (I'll spare you all the gory romantic details of the proposal, the wedding, etc.), we moved across town to live in his mansion.

Yup. That's right. His mansion.

Can you believe it? I, Kristy Thomas, actually live in a mansion. It's *huge*: three stories high, nine bedrooms. The living room (which is practically bigger than my old house) has floor-to-ceiling windows that look out on the humongous front lawn (where I was sitting that afternoon) and is big enough to hold a grand piano, three couches, five armchairs, a long glass coffee table, and an incredible crystal chandelier. And that's just the living room. I haven't even started to tell you about Watson's library.

Don't misunderstand; I'm not boasting. Things like chandeliers really aren't important to me at all. I'm just trying to give you an idea of my surroundings.

Okay, back to my family. As I said, I have two older brothers: Charlie, who's seventeen and has his driver's license, and Sam, who's fifteen and thinks about nothing but girls. Then there's David Michael, who's seven. He was only a baby when my father left, and since my mom was always working after that, I spent mondo hours caring for David Michael. I learned most of my baby-sitting skills during that time, so I guess I can thank David Michael for the fact that I'm now president of a very successful business called the Baby-sitters Club, or BSC (more about that later).

When Mom married Watson, he came with something extra: two kids from his first marriage. I love my stepsister and stepbrother. Their names are Karen and Andrew, and they are seven and four. Karen has an imagination the size of Texas and is a total live wire. Andrew is sweet and shy. The two of them live with us every other month, traveling back and forth from their mother's house to ours along with Bob the hermit crab and Emily Junior the rat. (Yes, she's named after Emily Michelle. Cute, no?)

Speaking of Emily Michelle, her arrival forced Mom and Watson to think about having someone in to help out with child care. That someone turned out to be Nannie, my mom's mother. She arrived in style in her old car — known as the Pink Clinker — and she dotes on all of us, whenever she's not too busy bowling or gardening or volunteering at the hospital. (She's another live wire.)

Is that everyone? I think so, though I haven't told you about Boo-Boo, Watson's way old, way cranky cat, or Crystal Light the Second and Goldfishie, the swimming pets. And you've already met Shannon, who is a Bernese mountain dog puppy. I never thought I'd have a purebred — our last dog (my beloved Louie) was a sort-of collie whose grandfather was a sheepdog — but Shannon was a gift our family couldn't refuse.

"Sannie!" Emily Michelle exclaimed suddenly, interrupting my Indian-summer daydreaming.

I sat up quickly, wondering why Emily Michelle was calling Shannon's name. Had the puppy wandered off? No, she was sleeping peacefully next to me, tail curled to touch her nose.

"Sannie!" Emily Michelle said again, and I looked up just in time to see what she was pointing at. Barreling toward us at what seemed like the speed of light was an in-line skater dressed in purple Lycra. She had thick blonde curls and she was outfitted with a helmet plus knee and elbow guards and wrist protectors, all in a shocking shade of pink. Towing her was a giant-sized version of Shannon, a strong, barrel-chested, brown-and-black dog with white markings. The dog's tongue hung out and I could swear she was grinning as she galumphed along happily.

The girl, however, wasn't exactly grinning. In fact, she looked terrified. "Help!" she cried. "Grab her!"

I jumped to my feet, ready for action. But as it turned out, there was no need to grab the dog. It stopped short as soon as it had reached its objective: Shannon. A tender nose-touch, some maternal snuffling, and the mother-daughter reunion was under way.

That's right. The big dog was Astrid, Shannon's mother. And, just to totally confuse you, the girl was Shannon. Shannon Kilbourne, that is. The *human* Shannon on our block. Bewildered? I don't blame you. I would be, too. Perhaps I should back up and explain.

See, when I first moved to Watson's house, I felt a little out of place. After all, this is a very wealthy neighborhood. And I thought the kids who lived here were snobby, especially Shannon, who paraded around with her purebred dog (Astrid's full name is Astrid of Grenville) and made fun of Louie, who was becoming very old and sick. But before long we'd become friends despite ourselves. We ironed out our misunderstandings, and as a peace offering Shannon gave my family one of Astrid's puppies. (Louie had been put to sleep by then and we missed him terribly.) David Michael promptly named the puppy after Shannon. I could have told him it would be confusing, but he was determined to have his way.

Now Shannon (the human) is a good friend and a member of the BSC, while Shannon (the puppy) is a much-loved member of the Thomas-Brewer family.

At that moment, the canine Shannon looked perfectly happy as she tumbled around under Astrid's gentle paw prods. But the other Shannon didn't look happy at all.

"Astrid," she called. "Come on. We only have ten minutes to finish our exercise!"

Astrid didn't even look up. Shannon (the human) gave an exasperated sigh.

"What's the rush?" I asked.

Shannon sighed again and shook her head. "This isn't working," she said. "I thought it would be efficient to combine my exercise with Astrid's afternoon walk, but she's distracted way too easily. I'm not getting any aerobic workout at all."

"So?" I said. "Just enjoy the time with Astrid and go skating by yourself later."

"I'd love to," said Shannon, "but there's no way I'll have time. Tonight I have to finish planning the next Astronomy Club meeting, plus write up the minutes for French Club. Also, I have to think about a presentation for Honor Society and make some calls about the All-Stoneybrook Dance. And I need to work on memorizing some lines. I'm auditioning for the school play."

This all came out in such a rush I could hardly follow what she said. But I understood the gist of it: Shannon was majorly busy. This is nothing new. Shannon is *always* busy. She's the student version of a workaholic, always signing up for more clubs, more activities, more extra-credit work. I don't know how she does it, especially when you consider that she's also a member of the BSC and makes all A's. (Shannon goes to Stoneybrook Day School, a private school). Plus, she helps out with the care of her two younger sisters, Tiffany and Maria.

"How are plans for the dance coming?" I asked. Shannon is the SDS representative for the All-Stoneybrook Dance committee. My friends and I are psyched about the dance they're planning, which is a first for our area. It's going to be a combined bash for the middle school kids at three schools: SDS, SMS, and Kelsey. It should be a blast.

Shannon rolled her eyes. "Don't ask about the dance," she said. "We have so much to do, and it's only a few weeks away. It's a madhouse."

I felt a little sorry for Shannon. Being on the committee should be fun, but it seemed as if she felt too overwhelmed to enjoy it. I thought for a second about a time when I was overbooked with responsibilities and remembered how anxious and tense I'd felt. I opened my mouth to suggest something to Shannon about cutting back (as I said, I'm never shy about giving my opinion), but before I could say a word she had grabbed Astrid's leash and was taking off down the street.

"See you!" she called, waving as she rolled away. "Nice talking to you." Her voice was already faint, and soon she disappeared around the corner. I shook my head, thinking what a shame it was to be so busy on such a beautiful day. Then I gave Emily Michelle a squeeze, stroked Shannon's soft ears, and lay in the leaves again to soak up some more of that warm October sun.

CHAPTER 2

"**H**ey! Your Royal Cluelessness!"

I looked up with a start. "Charlie!" I said. My brother was standing over me, grinning and shaking his head.

"I've been calling your name for the last five minutes, you airhead," he said. "Are you spacing out?"

"I guess I am," I admitted. The warm sun, Emily Michelle's sleepy yawns as she lay across my lap, the cozy autumn smell of leaves — all of it had made me so relaxed I'd forgotten everything else.

"Well, your space days are over," said Charlie, showing me his watch. "If we don't hustle, Madame President will be clocking in late."

"What?" I shouted, jumping to my feet. "It can't *really* be five-fifteen."

"Wanna bet?" asked Charlie. "Come on, let's move it. Nannie's inside waiting for Emily, the car's running, and Abby's on her way over — "

"No, Abby's here," interrupted Abby Stevenson, my neighbor and the most recent addition to the BSC. She'd appeared just as Charlie spoke her name. "And she's ready to go too, which is more than she can say for some people," she added teasingly.

"I don't believe this," I muttered as I sprinted across the yard, holding a still-sleepy Emily in my arms. "I'm *never* late. Never."

It's true. I'm never late for BSC meetings. After all, I have a reputation to maintain. As president, I insist on punctuality. A good sitter is never late for a job, not to mention a club meeting.

Inside, I unloaded Emily into Nannie's lap and gave each of them a quick kiss and a wave good-bye. Then I raced outside again, jumped into Charlie's car, and pulled the door shut with a slam. "Let's go!" I told Charlie. "What are you waiting for?"

He laughed as he shifted the car into gear. With a loud clunk, several sick-sounding coughs, and a strange squeal, the Junk Bucket (that's what we call Charlie's car, for obvious reasons) began to move.

I think the Junk Bucket could probably find its own way to Claudia Kishi's house by now. Charlie has driven me over there and back, three times a week, ever since we moved across town to Watson's house. (Before we moved, I could make it on my own to Claudia's. I grew up in the house across the street from hers.)

I guess now is the time to explain a little more about the BSC. We are a group of baby-sitters who meet every Monday, Wednesday, and Friday from five-thirty until six. Why? Pretend you're a parent who needs a reliable, experienced, responsible baby-sitter for next Thursday at seven. Would you rather make a bunch of calls to sitters you've never met, trying to find someone who *might* be free and *might* be trustworthy, or would you prefer to make one call to an established business that can guarantee you the kind of sitter you're looking for?

Right. Well, plenty of *real* parents feel the same way, which is why the BSC is the success that it is. It's such a simple idea, really. Anyone could have thought of it. But they didn't.

I did.

Which is why I'm president.

Let me just say now, without meaning to brag, that if there is one thing I'm very good at, it's having ideas. And having the energy and the drive to follow through on those ideas. You might call me pushy, you might call me bossy, but one thing you can never call me is lazy.

My friends aren't lazy either. In fact, I have to say that, while the rest of the BSC members aren't quite as busy as Shannon, not one of them is what you'd call a couch potato. All of us are active, busy people with very full lives. In a way, I think that's what makes us great sitters. We're just not interested in plopping down in front of the TV with our charges. We want to be *doing* things.

Take Claudia Kishi, for example. She's the vice-president of the BSC. We meet in her room because she has her own phone with a private line, which is essential for our business. Claudia is totally gorgeous, with long black hair and almond-shaped eyes. (Claudia is Japanese-American.) She's also crammed with talent, from the tips of her hand-painted sneakers to the tops of her creative hairdos.

Claudia may not be a world-class student. In fact, she's in the process of repeating seventh grade because eighth turned out to be more than she could handle, but she shines when it comes to art. (Her older sister, Janine, is the opposite. She's creatively challenged but a genius when it comes to academics.) Claudia's sculptures are stupendous. Her drawings are dumbfounding. And her paintings are prime. In short, she's an awesome artist. (Class, take note: All of the above are examples of alliteration. There will be a quiz tomorrow.)

Claud's creativity even extends to her outfits (they're wild), her Kid-Kit (a box of fun stuff she brings to sitting jobs; Claudia's is decorated differently each month), her room (full of art projects, art books, and art supplies), and even her hiding places. Hiding places? Yup, for books and munchies. Claudia's parents aren't crazy about her choice of reading material (Nancy Drew mysteries) or her choice of *eating* material (the junkiest of junk foods). So if you check any nook or cranny in Claudia's room, you're likely to turn up a couple of paperbacks or a Snickers bar.

Claudia's best friend, Stacey McGill, is another busy baby-sitter. She's the club's treasurer, which is a perfect job for someone with Stacey's natural talent for math. (We pay dues into the treasury every Monday and use the money to pay for things like Claud's phone bill and gas for the Junk Bucket.) Stacey is an only child who lives with her mom (her parents divorced not long ago). Her dad still lives in Manhattan, where Stacey grew up, so Stacey visits him as often as possible. That's not a hardship for her. Stacey ♥ NY. I think she'll always be a New Yorker at heart, and I know she'll always *look* like one. Stacey has long, curly blonde hair, blue eyes, and a sophisticated sense of style that tells you loud and clear that she's not from Stoneybrook.

(I haven't told you much about my style, which is basically nonexistent. I wear the same thing nearly every day: jeans, running shoes, and a turtleneck. I switch to shorts and T-shirts in the summer.)

Another thing that keeps Stacey busy is her diabetes. Imagine having to keep track of every single thing you eat (and avoiding any goodies like those Snickers bars of Claud's), having to give yourself frequent blood tests, and having to inject yourself with insulin on a regular basis. That's what Stacey has to do because she's diabetic. Diabetes is a lifelong condition that has to do with the way your body processes (or doesn't process) sugars. Stacey works hard to stay on top of her health, and I admire her for it. It can't be easy.

Abby Stevenson is another BSC member who has to spend time dealing with her health. Abby has allergies and asthma, and both problems require some attention. But her health isn't the only thing that keeps Abby busy, and it certainly doesn't slow her down. Abby is a natural athlete who loves any kind of physical activity. She runs, she plays tennis, she skis, she's on the soccer team — you name it, Abby does it, and she does it well. (I'm so impressed with her skills that I've even given her the supreme honor of making her the assistant manager for my little-kids' softball team, Kristy's Krushers.)

Abby and her twin sister, Anna, who have dark eyes and dark, curly hair, moved to my neighborhood recently. (They used to live on Long Island.) They live with their mother, who is an editor at a big publishing company in New York. Their father died several years ago in a car crash. Abby doesn't talk about him much, but I know she'll never stop missing her dad.

When the twins moved here, we asked both of them to be in the BSC, but Anna said she couldn't. She's way too busy with her music. Anna is an amazing violin player who puts most of her energy into practicing and playing. And until recently, she and Abby were also very busy studying and planning for their Bat Mitzvah, which is a Jewish celebration of a girl's transition to womanhood.

I am glad that Abby said yes to the BSC. She and I have had our clashes — we both have pretty strong personalities — but overall I'd have to say she's brought a breath of fresh air to the club. She's smart and quick and very, very funny. She's one of the best mimics I've ever seen. (You should see her imitation of our assistant principal, Mr. Kingbridge.)

Mary Anne Spier, my best friend and the secretary of the BSC, doesn't necessarily like Abby's imitations. She always feels bad for the person being imitated. Mary Anne's ultra-sensitive, ultra-gentle (am I making her sound like facial tissue?), and the best friend anyone could ever have. In a way, I think that's what keeps Mary Anne busiest: being a good friend. That may sound crazy, unless you know someone like her. Someone who really listens to what you have to say. Someone who calls you up when she knows you're feeling down. Someone who is always willing to do a friendly favor.

Being that kind of friend can be time-consuming.

Mary Anne and I may be opposites in temperament (nobody ever called me ultra-gentle!), but that's never kept us from being best friends. We actually look a little alike, but she pays more attention to fashion than I do. Mary Anne has a steady boyfriend, Logan Bruno, and a kitten she adores, named Tigger. Because she's neat and tidy and well-organized, she makes a terrific secretary for the BSC. She's in charge of our record book, which contains all our schedules as well as information about each of our clients.

I've been friends with Mary Anne forever, but I don't remember her mother. Neither does Mary Anne. That's because her mom died when Mary Anne was just a baby, leaving Mr. Spier to bring up their only child on his own. He did a good job of it, but he was very over-protective and treated Mary Anne like a little kid for way too long. He's much better since he fell in love and married again, giving Mary Anne not only a stepmother she loves but a new sister and brother as well.

The sister, Dawn Schafer, is another best friend to Mary Anne and was in the BSC until she recently moved back to California. That part is a little complicated, but let me explain. See, Dawn and her younger brother, Jeff, grew up in California, but their mom, Sharon, was originally from Stoneybrook. When she and Dawn's father divorced, Sharon and the kids moved back East, where she fell in love all over again with her high school sweetheart, Richard Spier (Mary Anne's dad). That's how Mary Anne and Dawn ended up as sisters. But Jeff and Dawn never adjusted to life in Connecticut, and over time both of them moved back to California to live with their dad. We all miss Dawn, Mary Anne most of all.

By the way, when Dawn was in the BSC, she was our alternate officer. That meant she could fill in for anybody who couldn't make it to a meeting. Our new alternate officer is Abby.

We also have two junior officers, Jessi Ramsey and Mallory Pike. While the rest of us are thirteen, Jessi and Mal are eleven. They take a lot of our afternoon sitting jobs. And, even though they're younger than the rest of us, they're just as busy. Jessi, who has dark hair and chocolate-brown skin, lives with her parents, her aunt, a little sister, and a baby brother. She's a talented ballet dancer who practices every day and takes tons of lessons.

Mal, who has reddish-brown hair and wears glasses, comes from a much larger family. She has seven younger brothers and sisters! As if that doesn't keep her busy enough, she also loves to read and write. (She's the only BSC member who truly enjoys making entries in our BSC notebook, where we write up each job we go on.) For now, Mallory mostly writes in her journal. Someday, though, she hopes to be an author-illustrator of children's books.

You may be wondering where Shannon, the Queen of Busyness, fits in, since I've mentioned that she's a BSC member. Well, she's what we call an associate member. She and the other associate member (Logan Bruno, Mary Anne's boyfriend) don't come to all our meetings, but they do help out with jobs when we're overbooked.

Shannon wasn't at our meeting that afternoon, of course. But her name came up. Why? Because one of our first calls was from her mom. It turned out that Mrs. Kilbourne had decided to join Shannon on the dance committee as a parent representative.

"Also," she said, "I've decided to take some classes at Stoneybrook University. I'm thinking about going back to school to work toward a teaching degree."

I raised my eyebrows. Shannon wasn't the only busy one in her family. "How can we help out?" I asked Mrs. Kilbourne.

"I'll need a sitter for Tiffany and Maria," she said, "several afternoons a week."

I told Mrs. Kilbourne we'd call her back. Mary Anne checked the record book, and we discussed who would be best for the job. Since the Kilbournes live in my neighborhood, and since Abby — who also lives nearby — has soccer practice nearly every afternoon these days, guess who signed on for the part.

That's right. I now had a steady job to look forward to. No more afternoons in the sun, at least for awhile. But, hey, since all my friends are so busy, I might as well be too. Right?

CHAPTER 3

"Kristy, you're a lifesaver," said Mrs. Kilbourne as she threw on her jacket and grabbed her car keys from the hall table. "The girls just came home from school, and they're in the kitchen, having a snack." She stood very still for a moment, and I could tell she was checking off items on a little list in her head. You know, the kind of list that goes, *Jacket. Keys. Greet Kristy. Leave.* Then she gave a quick sigh, called, "Good-bye, girls!" and sped out the door.

It was Tuesday, the day after our meeting, and my job at the Kilbournes' had begun. It was another gorgeous fall day, but this time I wouldn't be lying around in the leaves. I'd be working. And I was prepared. I'd brought my Kid-Kit. I'd brought some new books I thought might interest Tiffany and Maria. And I'd brought a great attitude and plenty of energy. I haven't done much sitting for Maria and Tiffany, and since this job was going to be regular, I thought it would be wise to make a good start.

I poked my head into the kitchen. Maria and Tiffany were seated at the kitchen table, wearing identical SDS uniforms (gray sweater-vests, white shirts, gray-and-green plaid skirts) and identical bored expressions. No, they are not twins. Not even close. Tiffany's eleven and has the same blonde hair, blue eyes (framed with long, dark lashes), and high cheekbones as her mom and older sister. Maria is eight. Her coloring is totally different, more like her dad's. Her hair is reddish-brown — auburn, I guess you call it — and her eyes are a dark hazel color, almost brown.

"Hey!" I said, greeting the girls with a big smile.

"Hi, Kristy," said Maria.

"Hi," echoed Tiffany.

Neither of them sounded all that thrilled to see me.

"I was really looking forward to coming over here today," I said, seating myself at the table. I plunked my Kid-Kit down in front of me. The girls barely gave it a glance.

"That's good," said Tiffany.

Maria didn't say anything. She just helped

herself to another Ritz cracker, then carefully spread it with peanut butter and began to nibble away.

"How's swim team?" I asked her. Maria-as-jock is a new thing. Until recently, she was pretty much a bookworm. Now she loves sports, especially swimming. Once I saw her swim in a neighbor's pool, and she was awesome. She's a much, much better swimmer than I am, that's for sure. She's like a dolphin in the water. And she's always excited about some upcoming meet.

But you wouldn't have known that by the way she answered me. "All right, I guess," she said without looking up.

"Are you still the backstroke champ?" I asked.

She nodded, but she didn't smile. What was with her? I tried one more question. "Any major meets coming up?"

She blinked. "Not for awhile," she said indistinctly. Her mouth was full of crackers and peanut butter.

I didn't want to keep bugging her if she didn't want to talk, so I turned to Tiffany. "How about you?" I asked. "What's new in your garden?" Tiffany is the Kilbourne family gardener. She has this tiny plot of land out back that she does amazing things with. It's packed with flowers and vegetables. Tiffany's a garden expert. And she loves to share her knowledge and enthusiasm.

Usually.

But not today. She barely managed a shrug. "Nothing much," she said.

"I know, it's fall," I replied. "I guess that means you're mostly concentrating on next year's garden." I've seen some of Tiffany's garden plans. She puts her heart and soul into them. They include perfectly scaled pictures of the garden, with neatly labeled colored-pencil drawings that show each plant in its ideal place.

She gave that little half shrug again. "Uh-huh," she muttered.

Okay. I'm not dense. The message was coming through loud and clear. Neither of the younger Kilbournes wanted to talk. Not to me, not to each other, not to anyone. All they wanted to do was sit and sulk.

But why?

I know curiosity killed the cat, but I can't help myself. I always want to find out the whys and hows behind everything. I tried to give myself a little lecture. *Forget it,* I thought. *Whatever's wrong is none of your business. If they wanted your help they'd ask for it. But they don't. All they want is to be left alone.*

Right. That talk lasted for about two seconds. Then I couldn't resist trying one more tactic. "Hey, guys," I said, "check out what I brought." I reached into my Kid-Kit as I spoke and pulled out items. "I found each of you something great to read," I said, holding out a book toward each girl.

"Already read it," said Tiffany.

"Hated it," said Maria.

"Okay." I tossed the books back into the box. "Then how about some stickers? Some new markers? A friendship-pin kit?" Desperately, I dumped my entire Kid-Kit onto the table.

Maria and Tiffany just looked at me.

"Stickers are for babies," said Tiffany.

"Those friendship pins are *so* last year," said Maria.

I blew out a sigh of exasperation. "What is *with* you guys? You don't want to talk. You don't want to do anything. You just sit there, looking like two bumps on a log. Listen," I went on. "I want the two of you to go upstairs and change out of your uniforms. Then come right back down. We're going to have a meeting." If I was going to sit regularly for Maria and Tiffany, something had to change. No way was I going to put up with their nasty moods for three long afternoons every single week.

For a second, I thought they were going to argue with me. Maria opened her mouth, then closed it. Tiffany frowned, started to say something, then frowned again. Then they stood up, pushed back their chairs, and headed upstairs.

It didn't take them long to change. Within ten minutes, both of them plodded back down the stairs. Maria had put on jeans and a blue sweatshirt. Tiffany was wearing overalls with a red turtleneck underneath. "Great," I said, eyeing them. "Now let's go sit in the TV room."

The Kilbournes have a spacious family room, just beyond the kitchen. It has a huge couch, a big TV, and a cabinet with glass shelves that are loaded with trophies and awards that Shannon and Maria have won. (If they gave trophies for gardening, Tiffany would have prizes up there too.) "Okay," I said. "Time to spill it. What's the matter?"

Maria coughed. Tiffany cleared her throat. But neither of them spoke.

"Come on," I said. "Out with it."

Another pause. Then Tiffany started to talk, and I thought she'd never stop. Maria joined in too. Both of them talked for a long, long time.

"We're mad at Shannon," said Tiffany. "And at our parents. Really mad. But we can't even talk to them about it because they're never here."

"They're all just way too busy," put in Maria. "And that's why we're mad."

"Nobody ever has time for us anymore," said Tiffany. "Mom never even asks what we did at school, or who we've been playing with.

Shannon always acts like she has more important things on her mind, if you want to talk to her. And Dad pays more attention to his beeper than he does to us."

Maria looked as if she were about to cry. "I don't care if Daddy *is* the main lawyer on a big case. I miss him. And I miss Mom. Why does she have to go to stupid old school?"

"The worst part is Shannon, though," said Tiffany. "She's always been busy before, but never like this. She used to have time for us, no matter what."

I listened to everything they said, and my heart ached for them. It was no wonder they were feeling sulky. "When was the last time your family had dinner together?" I asked gently.

Maria and Tiffany looked at each other and shook their heads. "I don't know," said Tiffany slowly. "A long, long time ago. That's for sure."

"I'm really sorry," I said, "but I'm glad you told me. You know why?"

"Why?" asked Maria warily.

"Because I'm going to help you figure out what to do about it."

"Do about it?" asked Maria. "What can we do about it? This is just the way things are."

"Maybe not," I said. I'd been thinking furiously, and I'd come up with an idea. I remembered how harried Shannon had seemed when she was trying to exercise and walk the dog at the same time. "Shannon has a lot to do right now," I said. "What if we thought about some ways to help her? What if you guys could save her some time?"

"That might work," said Maria.

"But how can we help?" asked Tiffany. "Most of what she does is for French Club or stuff like that. I don't know any French."

"Let's do some brainstorming," I suggested. "I bet we can come up with some ideas." I ran for my Kid-Kit and pulled out a pad of drawing paper I always keep handy. Then I sat down between Tiffany and Maria, pad and pen in hand. I was energized, and they were too. Together we were going to tackle this problem — and win.

CHAPTER 4

I thought our list looked great. So did the girls. Shannon was going to be one lucky big sister. Imagine having two wonderful siblings whose greatest wish was to make your life easier. What could be better? By the time I left the Kilbournes' that Tuesday, Maria and Tiffany were excited, and so was I. Operation SOS (for Save Our Sister) was going to change Shannon's life.

And it did.

But not in the way we'd intended.

Over the next few days, Maria and Tiffany worked their way down the list we'd made. They worked extra hard to help Shannon in every way possible. Every ounce of their energy went toward Operation SOS.

So what went wrong?

Just about everything. For starters, here's what happened with item number one on the list:

1. MAKE SHANNON'S FAVORITE COOKIES

Of course, making Shannon cookies wasn't exactly a helping-out kind of thing. But Tiffany insisted that it would be a great way to kick off their new plan. "Shannon loves Snickerdoodles so much," she explained. "And Mom never has time to make them anymore. If Shannon has a good supply of Snickerdoodles, she'll be happier. And if she's happier, that might mean she'll be nicer to us."

I had no idea what Snickerdoodles were, so Maria had to explain. "They're yummy," she said. "Not as yummy as brownies — those are my favorite — but they're definitely yummy. They're kind of buttery tasting and they have walnuts and raisins inside and cinnamon and sugar all over the outside." She rubbed her stomach. "Just thinking about them makes me hungry."

So that's what we did on Thursday. We made Snickerdoodles. Or at least we tried. I stayed in the background and let Maria and Tiffany take charge, since that was important to them. All I did was check with Mrs. Kilbourne to make sure it was okay for the girls to bake. Then I watched the whole disaster unfold.

As soon as they'd changed out of their uniforms, the girls tied on aprons, pulled out ingredients, and began to do the Betty Crocker thing.

"I told you to put the butter on the counter before we left for school!" Tiffany said to Maria. She had dropped a stick of butter — straight out of the fridge — into a bowl, and she was trying to mush it around with a big wooden spoon. The butter was basically un-mushable. I could hear it thudding against the sides of the bowl.

"I can't remember *everything*!" said Maria. "And for that matter, why didn't *you* remember to put raisins on Mom's shopping list? All we have are the ones left over from Christmas, and they're dried out."

"Raisins are supposed to be dried out," said Tiffany, still struggling with the butter.

"Not like this," said Maria. "This is *beyond* dried out. This raisin is practically mummi-fied."

"Well, what do you want me to do about it now? We're just going to have to use them, mummified or not." Tiffany poked at the stick of butter again, and it flew out of her bowl and onto the floor. She let out a howl.

"Hey, you guys, pipe down!" Shannon yelled from upstairs. "I'm tired of hearing you bicker. Why don't you go outside and fight in-stead?"

Maria and Tiffany quieted down instantly.

The cookies were supposed to be a surprise. If Shannon came into the kitchen to see what they were doing, that would ruin everything.

"I have an idea," I said gently. "How about if we microwave the butter for a couple of seconds? That ought to soften it up. And Maria, maybe if we pour some hot water over the raisins they'll plump up a little."

I may not be one of the great chefs of all time, but I've baked more than a few batches of cookies.

The girls welcomed my ideas, and, working cooperatively, they soon turned out a lovely batch of cookies.

I wish.

In fact, what happened was that after a brief peaceful period, the girls went back to squabbling. Shannon had left for a French Club meeting, so it didn't matter so much. Still, they paid so much attention to fighting that the cookie-making was a disaster. One batch burned. Another batch stuck to the pan. There were no raisins left for a third batch. (P.S. Naturally, as a responsible baby-sitter, I was the one operating the oven.)

Meanwhile, the kitchen was taking on the look of one of those *I Love Lucy* episodes in which everything goes wrong. There was cookie dough everywhere — on the faucets, on the oven knobs, on the refrigerator door handle, even on the ceiling. (Don't ask me how it ended up there.) Flour dusted every surface, walnuts crunched underfoot, and the sink was overflowing with bowls, spatulas, baking sheets, and measuring spoons.

Mrs. Kilbourne came home just as I was pulling the fourth batch (minus raisins *and* nuts) out of the oven. She stood in the middle of the kitchen and surveyed the mess. Her face was pale. "What — " she asked weakly.

"Snickerdoodles," explained Tiffany in a tiny voice.

Mrs. Kilbourne rolled her eyes. "I guess you've both forgotten that you have plans for tonight," she said. She pointed at the clock. "We have to be out of here in five minutes!"

Tiffany clapped a hand over her mouth. "Oh, no," she said. "You're right. I'm supposed to go over to Martha's house to work on our science project."

"And I have a swim team meeting!" said Maria. She glanced around at the kitchen. "What are we going to do?"

Her mother frowned. "I'm going to have to ask Shannon to take care of it," she said. "She's the only one who'll be at home tonight, since Daddy and I have a dinner party to go to."

Maria and Tiffany exchanged an anguished look. I knew I should clean up, but the fact was I couldn't. I'd promised my mom I'd cook dinner that night. "See you tomorrow," I said, waving to the distraught girls.

What a disaster.

2. WALK ASTRID

Another disaster. This time, it seemed as if nothing could go wrong. What was simpler than walking a dog? And what could be more helpful? After all, Shannon was having a hard time fitting Astrid's walks into her schedule. And the dog belonged to the whole family. It made sense for Tiffany and Maria to take over her afternoon walk. Even Shannon, still a little sulky about the kitchen episode of the day before, had to agree.

"Just be careful when you go by the Papadakises'. If Astrid sees Noodle, she'll pull really hard," Shannon said as she dashed out of the house, on her way to the library.

Noodle is, in case you're wondering, a poodle.

"I know, I know," said Tiffany. "It's not like I never walked her before." She grabbed the leash, attached it to Astrid's collar, and opened the door. The three of us set out, full of that good feeling you can only earn by doing a good deed. It was another gorgeous, crisp fall day. Astrid's tail was up and waving gaily as she trotted along. I whistled the theme from *Be-*

witched. Maria and Tiffany chattered and giggled.

You can probably guess what happened next.

Before I knew it, we were passing the Papadakises'. I was just about to remind Tiffany to hold on tight to Astrid's leash when a white blur flashed in front of us.

"Noodle!" shouted Maria.

But Astrid had already figured that out. She gave one hard lunge and the leash snapped out of Tiffany's hand. Then Astrid was off and running — dashing through hedges, jumping over flower beds, dodging trees — all in pursuit of Noodle, who seemed to love the game.

"Astrid!" I called.

"Come, Astrid!" shouted Tiffany.

"Here, girl!" said Maria.

Nothing worked. It was as if she were deaf. Deaf and fast. In about three seconds, we'd lost sight of her. Tiffany stood there looking stunned, her empty hands by her sides. Maria burst into tears.

"They'll come back," I said, trying to sound positive.

"Noodle will," said Tiffany in a monotone. "But Astrid won't. Once she starts running, she hates to stop." Tiffany sounded as if she'd been through this before.

Sure enough, a couple of minutes later Noodle came trotting back. He stepped delicately up the stairs onto the Papadakises' porch and settled down for a nap. But Astrid was nowhere in sight.

"So, what do we do now?" I asked Tiffany.

"We walk around calling her. But there's really only one person who can tempt her into coming back," she said sadly.

"And that would be — ?" I asked, almost not wanting to know.

"Shannon," the girls said together.

3. HELP SHANNON WITH HOMEWORK

I had wondered about this one from the start. And I should have said something about my doubts. But I didn't, so it's probably my fault that it all went so wrong.

I guess it happened over the weekend, when I wasn't around. The first I heard of it was on Monday afternoon, when I showed up to sit for Maria and Tiffany. They'd just come home from school, as usual, and were sitting at the kitchen table in their uniforms, having a snack, as usual. Everything seemed peaceful, and I was just about to ask how Operation SOS had gone over the weekend when I heard thundering footsteps coming down the stairs.

A second later, Shannon burst into the kitchen, waving a sheaf of papers. "How *could* you?" she shouted.

Tiffany and Maria stared at her. "What?" asked Maria innocently.

"My algebra homework. You turned it into utter nonsense!" Shannon said angrily. "This was the most embarrassing day I ever had at school."

"We were just trying to help," said Tiffany in a small voice. "We know you don't have much time, and — "

"Trying to help?" asked Shannon. "How? By changing every *x* to a number? Don't you understand? Algebra is *supposed* to have *x's*."

"It just didn't look right," said Maria. "It seemed wrong to have letters in there with all the numbers."

"Well, it wasn't. It was right," said Shannon. "And it wasn't easy to explain my mistakes to Ms. Crifo — in front of the entire class." She turned on her heel to leave, then turned back for one last word. "Next time you want to 'help' somebody, do her a favor and just stay away."

Ouch.

I can't believe we had the nerve to keep trying after that, but we did. I still thought it would all work out and that Shannon would discover how much her sisters cared. That's why we tried one last item on our list:

4. CLEAN SHANNON'S ROOM

I won't even go into the gory details. Just imagine a malfunctioning vacuum cleaner that blows out instead of sucking in — and a pile of carefully arranged French Club notes. Imagine trying to dust with upholstery cleaner instead of Lemon Pledge. Imagine washing windows with a greasy rag. I think you'll understand why the room-cleaning disaster was the last straw.

I don't remember much about what Shannon said when she came home later that afternoon, but I have no problem recalling the general ideas she outlined. The thrust of her message was that Tiffany and Maria were the biggest pests she'd ever seen and that she'd prefer it if they'd stay out of her room, her business — and her face.

She wasn't nasty about it. She was calm and rational and even told them she still loved them. But she left no doubt in her sisters' minds.

Operation SOS had been a total failure.

CHAPTER 5

Monday

Such exitmint! I havent seen the kids so wound up in a long, long time. I think this event will be a real winner — that is, if we can ever get the comm— mitte to agree on enything. and thats a big if.

It was the Monday after the room-cleaning catastrophe. I was sitting for Maria and Tiffany again, and Claudia had a job over at the Kormans', who live just next door to the Kilbournes. She was sitting for Bill, who's nine, Melody, who's seven, and Skylar, the baby, who's only one-and-a-half. I like the Korman kids a lot. Since they live in my neighborhood, I've done lots of sitting for them, and by now I know them pretty well. Melody and Bill go to Stoneybrook Day, and Melody is good friends with my stepsister, Karen.

As it turned out, Claudia and I and our charges ended up hanging out together that day — along with a bunch of other kids. When I arrived at the Kilbourne house I found two very bummed-out little girls. Maria and Tiffany were upset about the failure of Operation SOS, and I couldn't blame them. I couldn't figure out how to cheer them up either. Not until my latest Great Idea came to me, that is.

The idea hit me when Shannon and Mrs. Kilbourne left that afternoon for an All-Stoneybrook Dance committee meeting. Maria and Tiffany, who were still in their school uniforms, sat at the kitchen table, picking glumly at their afternoon snack.

"Who cares about that dumb old dance anyway?" Maria asked. "I don't know why

Mommy and Shannon are so excited about it."

"I know," said Tiffany. "It's just a stupid dance."

The girls felt left out. It was too bad the dance was only for middle school kids. But if the younger kids had their own dance . . . "Hey!" I exclaimed. "Why couldn't there be an All-*Kids* Dance?"

I saw a spark of interest in Maria's and Tiffany's eyes. But it only lasted an instant. "Mom's too busy to plan that too," said Maria.

"She doesn't have to," I said. "We can do it ourselves."

Tiffany was nodding. "We could, you know," she said. "How hard could it be?"

Famous last words, right? Well, maybe. But I was so excited by the idea that I plowed ahead. "I'm going to call Claudia," I said. "She's right next door at the Kormans'. Let's see if they want to be in on this. We could have our first meeting right now!"

My enthusiasm was contagious. Maria and Tiffany started to chatter about where the dance could be and when, and what they might wear to it.

I jumped up and grabbed the phone. "Claud, listen to this," I said. I explained the idea, and she loved it. She, in turn, told Bill and Melody.

"Come on over," she said. "We're not doing anything."

By the time we arrived at the Kormans', Claudia and her charges had already started planning. "Look!" said Bill, pointing to pens and pads laid out on the huge kitchen table. "We're all set for a meeting."

"Great," I said. "But how come there are so many chairs at the table?"

"Because the Kormans and Kilbournes go to Stoneybrook Day, but we'll need representatives from other schools," Claudia explained. "Bill and Melody and I have been on the phone nonstop, and a bunch of other kids are on their way over."

"Wow," I said, overwhelmed. Usually I'm the one pushing plans along. This idea already had a life of its own. "Where's Skylar?" I asked.

"Upstairs with Mrs. Korman," Claudia said. "She's not feeling too well, so she stayed home. She said it was okay if other kids come over as long as things are quiet. Skylar has a slight fever."

Just then, the doorbell rang. "I'll get it!" cried Melody.

"Not without me, you won't," said Claudia, laughing, as she raced to the door with Melody. One of our BSC rules is that we never let charges answer the door alone, even if we're expecting someone.

Claudia opened the door and found two of the Papadakis kids. They'd walked over, since they live just two houses down from the Kormans. (They're the ones who own Noodle the Poodle, remember?) And they go to Stoneybrook Academy, which is a private elementary school — the one Karen goes to. Hannie is seven, and she has an olive complexion with dark hair and eyes, and the quickest smile I've ever seen. Linny is nine, with similar looks. He also smiles a lot. The Papadakis kids are very good-natured.

Just as they were arriving, an old Volkswagen pulled up and Becca Ramsey (Jessi's eight-year-old sister) and Charlotte Johanssen (Becca's neighbor and best friend, also eight) jumped out. Karen also came over. By then I'd joined Claudia at the door, and she and I waved to Becca's aunt Cecelia, who'd driven the girls over, and called, "Thanks!" She waved back and drove off.

Next to arrive was Triple Trouble — the Pike triplets, Jordan, Adam, and Byron, who are ten years old. Mrs. Pike dropped them off on her way to the grocery store. I noticed this relieved smile on her face as she drove off. The triplets can be a handful. They're probably easier to deal with now that they're ten and can do a lot for themselves. I often wonder how Mrs. Pike made it through those early years when the boys were babies and Mal was just a toddler.

They bounded up the walkway and shoved each other aside in their haste to be first inside. "Out of my way, booger head," said Adam, elbowing Byron.

"Move it or lose it," said Jordan, giving Adam a push in the shoulder.

"Beep, beep, coming through!" yelled Byron, shoving both of them out of the way.

Claudia and I exchanged looks over their heads, rolling our eyes. This meeting was going to be a circus.

Surprisingly, it started off fairly well. Tiffany had somehow decided she was in charge. Once everyone had grabbed a paper cup of juice (Melody passed them around) and a handful of cookies (Bill handed those out), Tiffany shouted — to make herself heard over the din — that everybody should take a seat.

"I hereby bring this meeting of the All-Kids Dance committee to order," she called. She looked down at her pad of paper, which she'd already filled with notes (a president after my own heart!), and went on. "We have representatives from each school here. Linny, Hannie, and Karen are all from Stoneybrook Academy. Stoneybrook Day is represented by Melody, Bill, Maria, and me. And Charlotte, Becca, and you guys — " she swept a hand toward the Pike boys — "are all from Stoneybrook Elementary."

"We know, we know," said Adam.

"This is *bor*ing," sang Jordan.

Tiffany silenced him with a Look. "Did I just hear you volunteer for the decorations committee, Jordan?" she asked.

Jordan looked sheepish. "No," he mumbled, "but I guess I will."

"Who says there's even going to *be* a decorations committee?" asked Linny. "Can we back up and figure some things out? Like, where's the dance going to be?"

"SES!" shouted all three Pikes at once. "No way it could be anywhere else," added Jordan. "Our school gym rules."

"I bet you've never even seen Stoneybrook Academy's gym," Hannie said. "It's really nice."

Actually, I could barely even hear Hannie over the argument that had broken out between Bill, Adam, and Karen. They were shouting at each other at the top of their lungs, each insisting that their school was the best place for a dance. Charlotte and Becca looked a little taken aback by all the yelling. They shrank into their seats as if they'd like to hide.

I stuck two fingers into my mouth and gave the loudest whistle I'm capable of. I bet Astrid heard it, even with all the windows closed.

The kids fell silent and looked up at me.

"Whoa," I said quietly. "Slow down. This isn't a war between the schools. This is a fun event, one you're all going to share in." I caught my breath, ready to go on with my lecture, but Tiffany jumped in.

"Kristy's right," she said. "I'm sure we can plan this without fighting. How about if we talk about all the different stuff we'll have to plan and then figure out who's going to take care of each area. Like, we have to think about food and music — " As she spoke, she made notes on her pad.

Tiffany was acting like a leader. The kids felt it too, and they responded. "We have to figure out when the dance is going to be," pointed out Becca.

"And how to let kids know it's happening," added Adam.

Tiffany nodded, adding items to her list. "Right," she said.

Soon the suggestions were flying — but nobody was fighting, nobody was yelling. Claudia and I glanced at each other and smiled. The All-Kids Dance was going to happen and it was going to be great.

"The only thing that worries me," Claudia said to me later that day as we waited for the others to arrive at our BSC meeting, "is the way the kids kept glancing at each other. I have the feeling they may be worried about something connected with the dance, like — " she paused.

"Like, dates?" I asked. I'd sensed the same unease. "I know. I saw Linny looking at Charlotte, and I could practically hear the wheels turning inside his head. 'How can I ask her? What if she says no?' Poor kid." I shook my head. "We'll have to talk to them about that."

Claudia agreed. "Speaking of dates," she said casually, "how would you like one for the dance?"

"What?" I asked, shocked.

"Mark knows this guy from Kelsey, an eighth-grader who's really into sports. I think you guys would have a blast together." Claudia looked at me hopefully. Mark is her seventh-grade sort-of boyfriend. I don't know him very well, since seventh- and eighth-graders don't mix too much. Claud is so excited about being at a dance with us — her friends — *and* her boyfriend. I could see she really wanted me to say yes to this blind-date idea.

"I don't know," I said. Ugh. I hate the idea of going to a dance with someone I barely know. "Plus, Bart may be at the dance." Bart Taylor is a friend who used to be a little *more* than a friend, if you know what I mean.

"Right. He might even be there with someone else," Claud pointed out.

Double ugh. "Oh, okay," I said. "But I don't want the dance to be our first date. How about a trial run, so we can see if we even like each other?"

"Great idea!" Claudia said. She reached for the phone immediately and punched in Mark's number. "And I know you're going to be nuts about him. This is so excellent."

I rolled my eyes. What was I getting myself into?

CHAPTER 6

As it happened, I didn't see Maria and Tiffany for several days. (Mrs. Kilbourne had no classes, and the dance committee wasn't meeting.) And by the time I returned to the Kilbourne home, I discovered that war had broken out.

War?

That's right. A Sister War. Declared by Tiffany and Maria. The enemy? Shannon, of course.

I saw the document they'd drawn up, soon after the room-cleaning disaster.

DECLARATION OF WAR

We, the undersigned, do hereby declare war on our sister Shannon. We swear to do everything in our power to make her life miserable. The reason for this war is that

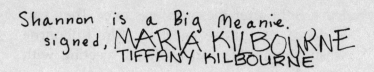

Shannon is a Big Meanie.
signed, MARIA KILBOURNE
TIFFANY KILBOURNE

The declaration of war was bad enough, but I nearly lost it when I saw the battle plans they'd drawn up. Like Operation SOS, it was in list form. But this time, the list wasn't full of lovely, sisterly acts. This time it included every nasty prank, obnoxious trick, and diabolical deed two little girls could possibly think up.

They really were going to make Shannon's life miserable.

And there was nothing I could do to stop them.

I tried, believe me. I told them their war wouldn't work if what they wanted was Shannon's attention and love. I told them it wasn't nice to treat their sister that way. And I told them I would do everything I could to make sure they didn't wage war during the times I was sitting for them.

They didn't care. They'd declared war and they were sticking with it. And I was on hand to see the very first battle.

1. DRIVE SHANNON CRAZY

It happened at dinner that night. Mrs. Kilbourne had asked me to stay after an afternoon of sitting since she and Shannon would have to leave right after the meal was over. They had a dance committee meeting. Mr. Kilbourne wasn't home. He had a dinner meeting with some clients.

It was going to be a quick, informal meal, but Mrs. Kilbourne still wanted everyone seated at the table. "Family dinners are important," she said. "And we don't have them nearly often enough."

I knew that was no lie, based on what Maria and Tiffany had told me. I took the seat Mrs. Kilbourne pointed out, between her and Shannon. Maria and Tiffany sat opposite us. Their chore had been to set the table, and now they waited while Mrs. Kilbourne filled their plates with microwaved lasagna and store-bought salad.

Once everyone had their food, we began to eat. Mrs. Kilbourne asked each of the girls what they'd done in school that day. Maria and Tiffany gave short, two-word answers. Shannon told a funny story about something that had happened in her math class, but neither of her sisters laughed. They just sat there poker-faced.

Then they started in. "Excuse me, but could you pass the Shannon?" Maria asked Tiffany politely.

Without so much as a blink, Tiffany passed Maria the salt.

"Shannon you," said Maria.

"You're Shannon," said Tiffany.

Shannon — the *actual* Shannon — just stared at them. Mrs. Kilbourne had given up on polite dinner conversation and was busy going over some lists as she ate. She barely seemed to notice what was going on.

Tiffany smiled at Maria. "Wasn't it a Shannon day today?" she asked. Maria nodded and smiled back.

Shannon frowned.

Maria took a large bite of lasagna. "This Shannon is absolutely Shannon, don't you think?" she asked her sister.

"Hey, guys," I said. "Come on. That's annoying."

"I agree," Tiffany said to Maria, ignoring me. "But don't Shannon with your Shannon full. It's rude."

By this time Shannon was gritting her teeth. "Cut it out, you two," she said.

"Shannon it out?" asked Tiffany. "Why?"

"Because I said so," said Shannon through pinched lips. "You're driving me nuts."

Maria and Tiffany looked at each other and grinned.

Turning their sister's name into a household word had been incredibly effective, and they kept it up all through dinner, until Mrs. Kilbourne finally caught on to what was happening and made them stop. After that, they simply whispered Shannon's name as the three sisters cleared the table and tidied the kitchen. Shannon did her best to ignore them, but Maria and Tiffany knew they'd gotten under her skin. The Sister War was on — and they were winning! Their first objective had already been met.

2. MESS UP SHANNON's SCHEDULE

I must say that Tiffany and Maria know their sister well. They had no trouble figuring out the best ways to aggravate Shannon. Three days after the scene at the dinner table, I was on hand to witness the results of the girls' next Sister War scheme.

I was sitting in the kitchen with Tiffany and Maria when Shannon walked in. It was a little unusual to see her home from school so early; normally she has at least two after-school activities.

She flopped into a chair and helped herself to a granola bar. "Whew, am I beat," she said. "I'm so happy I didn't have to stay too late at school today. You can go home now, Kristy."

I noticed her sisters exchanging a raised-eyebrow look. But before I could say anything, the phone rang.

Shannon jumped up to answer it. "Hello? . . .

Oh, hi, Nancy. . . . What? French Club? Today?"
She shook her head — as if the person on the other end of the line could see her — and went on. "Are you sure? I have it written down for tomorrow." She reached over and fumbled with her backpack, which was hanging on the back of the chair she'd been sitting in. In a moment, she pulled out a green datebook. She flipped through it. "Yes, definitely. I mean, *oui*. It's for tomorrow." She listened again. "Everybody else is there? Well, I guess I must have it wrong. I'll be there as soon as I can."

She put down the phone and looked at her sisters. "You don't have anything to do with this, do you?" she asked. "Or with the fact that I missed a lunchtime meeting of the Honor Society? Not to mention the Astronomy Club planning session I was supposed to attend yesterday?" She threw the datebook down on the table and put her hands on her hips.

Maria and Tiffany looked blank. "Us?" asked Tiffany innocently. "What could we have done?"

"We didn't do anything," Maria insisted. "You just have too many meetings all the time. You must have lost track."

"Right," said Shannon. "Look, you guys. Whether you admit it or not, I think you've been fooling around with my datebook. And I want you to stop. Now. I can't afford to miss these meetings. Not only is it embarrassing, but it might mean I end up being kicked out of one of my clubs." She didn't wait for excuses or answers. She just dumped her datebook into her backpack and walked out the door.

"Uh, guys?" I said. "I think she means it. And she's right. If you'd messed up one of her baby-sitting jobs, for example, we might have been pretty mad. The BSC doesn't put up with people missing jobs."

"We would never have done that!" blurted Maria. Then she clapped a hand over her mouth, realizing that she'd practically admitted that they *had* made all the other changes. "Oops," she said, looking at Tiffany.

Tiffany shrugged. "The Sister War isn't over yet," she said. She was unfazed and ready to carry on.

3. "FORGET" SHANNON'S PHONE MESSAGES
4. STEAL SHANNON'S HOMEWORK
5. HIDE SHANNON'S SHOES
6. SHORT-SHEET SHANNON'S BED
7. PUT SOAP ON SHANNON'S TOOTHBRUSH
8. HIDE SHANNON'S DEODERANT

9. MESS UP SHANNON'S SOCK DRAWER
10. PUT ITCHING POWDER IN SHANNON'S SHOES

By the end of that week, the Sister War was the main event at the Kilbournes' house. Tiffany and Maria had done everything on their list — and more. There was only one problem. Shannon was still ignoring them.

No matter what they did, she managed to keep her cool. She let them know how she felt about their pranks, but after that first night at the dinner table she never blew up at them. In fact, she barely acknowledged her sisters at all. Which meant just one thing:

Tiffany and Maria were losing the Sister War.

CHAPTER 7

"Excuse me, but have you seen my friend Kristy Thomas? She's the president of this club, and she's usually here by now — " Stacey looked down at her watch and then back at me, a bewildered expression on her face.

"Oh, give me a break," I said. "I don't look *that* different, do I?"

Stacey just stared at me. "Actually," she said, "you do."

Claudia grinned. "Cool," she said.

Of course she thought it was cool. She was the one responsible for my new look. Claudia and I had gone shopping that day.

That statement might not mean much to people who don't know me well. But for anyone acquainted with the real Kristy Thomas, those words could cause an advanced state of shock. Why? Because Kristy Thomas does not shop.

Especially not with someone like Claudia, the Queen of Style. Claudia and I exist in parallel universes as far as fashion is concerned. In her world, fashion rules. You are what you wear. In mine, fashion doesn't even register on the radar. The phrase "Big Sale on Accessories" means nothing to me.

But Claudia insisted on taking me shopping for a new outfit to wear on our double date. "Haven't you heard what they say about first impressions?" she asked me at school as we talked near my locker after the last bell had rung. "You're going to be meeting this guy for the very first time. Don't you want him to think you're cute?"

I didn't answer.

"Kristy?" asked Claudia.

"I'm thinking about it," I said. "And the fact is, no, I don't want him to think I'm *cute*. I want him to think I'm nice and smart and funny. Why should I care what he thinks of the way I dress?"

"It's not about the clothes," said Claud. "It's just about a way of presenting yourself. A way that says to other people, 'I'm special.' Like, see this jumper?"

"How could I not?" I said. Claudia's jumper was made out of an old pair of overalls, and it was decorated with embroidered birds, animals, suns, moons, and stars. Claud had done all the needlework herself, and even I had to admit it looked terrific. "It looks great. And even if I didn't know you, I'd be able to tell you are a creative person."

"My point exactly. Your clothes should say something about you. You can make a statement with what you wear."

"What statement am I making right now?" I asked, looking down at my forest green turtleneck, my blue jeans, and my old, beat-up running shoes.

Claudia paused, considering. "You're saying, 'I don't care too much about clothes.' "

"Bingo!" I said. Claudia looked crestfallen. In fact, she looked so bummed out that I had to give in. "But just to humor you," I went on, "I'll pretend to care a little bit, just this once. Deal?"

"Deal!"

And so our journey began.

"Can't we go to Bellair's?" I asked. It was three o'clock, and Claudia and I were sitting in the Junk Bucket, which was parked in our driveway. Claud had come home from school with me. She knew better than to let me out of her sight once I'd agreed to go shopping.

Claudia sighed. "I thought I explained this already," she said. "We go to the *mall*. Why?" She held up three fingers.

"For better variety," I said tiredly, and Claudia put down one finger. "For better bargains," I went on in a singsong voice. Claud put down another finger and raised her eyebrows. "And for fun," I said flatly. She put down the third finger and grinned. "As if," I said under my breath. Shopping, fun? Not on my planet.

Claudia ignored my attitude. "You're learning," she said cheerfully. "Besides, what could be more perfect? Charlie's going to the mall anyway. He'll take us there, then drive us straight to my house for our meeting. Believe me, once you see what shopping with an expert is like, you'll love it. You'll be begging me to take you again."

"Right," I said. "Sure." I sank down in my seat, trying to remind myself that Claudia meant well.

Charlie jumped into the driver's seat just then and fired up the engine. With a rattle and a cough, we were off. Unfortunately, the car ran fine for once and did not break down. We made it to Washington Mall in record time.

The mall is huge. It has five levels and more stores than you can imagine. I became well acquainted with the mall when my friends and I worked there for awhile as part of a special class at school called Project Work. I didn't have a job in a store, though. I was with Mall Security. I loved it, but I've never understood why some people consider it fun to hang around the mall, looking in store windows all afternoon. I'd rather be outside playing ball.

Claudia, on the other hand, probably considers the mall her second home. She sighed with contentment as we entered the main doors. "Here we are," she said happily. "Now, where to start? We'll walk the entire mall, if we have time," she said, as if there were no room for argument there. "But as always, there's only one question."

"About where we should eat?" I suggested.

"No," she said, shaking her head. "About whether we should go clockwise or counterclockwise. Stacey and I always disagree about whether it's better to start with Steven E. and move on toward Macy's or if it's more fun to start at Steven E. and go toward Lear's." She shrugged. "Well, we're starting at Steven E. in any case. So let's go. Shall we?" She made a mock bow and offered me her arm.

I rolled my eyes. "Let's not make a whole big production out of this, okay?" I asked. "Let's just find an outfit and be done with it." I started walking, and Claudia trotted after me.

"You just don't get it, do you?" she said, shaking her head. "It's fun. Really. You'll see."

I had my doubts about that, but I resolved to keep an open mind. After all, Claudia was trying to do me a favor. The least I could do was humor her.

Easier said than done.

It was hard to hide my feelings when we

walked into Steven E. "This is such a weird store," I said.

"It's not a store, it's a boutique."

"Uh-huh," I said. "I see." As far as I could tell, the difference between a store and a boutique was that A) the salespeople all looked like models and acted like royalty; B) there were only about five things on display: one perfect sweater, one perfect skirt, one perfect pair of gloves — well, you get the picture; and C) I felt an immediate need to turn and run.

Claudia insisted that we look around. "Just for inspiration," she whispered.

I picked up a plain white T-shirt that was lying, perfectly folded, on a beautiful antique table. "This isn't bad," I said, holding it up to show Claudia. She nodded. Great! If I could buy a T-shirt and make her happy, my job was over. I flipped over the price tag and nearly fainted.

The shirt cost seventy-nine dollars.

"We're out of here," I announced to Claudia. I didn't wait for a response. I just turned and left the store. Excuse me, *boutique*.

I knew there was no point in asking Claudia how a white T-shirt could possibly be worth seventy-nine dollars. It was just one of those fashion things I'll never understand. So I kept my mouth shut.

Next, Claudia led me on a forced march to

Macy's, with stops at some interesting stores along the way. Interesting, that is, by Claud's definition. Not mine. She didn't let me even look at the puppies in the window at Critters, the pet shop. She hustled me right past Donut Delite, ignoring my pleas for just one cruller. And she absolutely refused to let me stop in at the Cheese Outlet, where it's always fun and educational to try the free samples.

Claudia was on a mission. She was going to find me a new outfit if it killed her or drove us both crazy, which it very nearly did. Finally, though, we agreed on a flowered skirt, a soft fleecy vest, and a silky cream-colored blouse, all of which we found in the juniors' department at Macy's.

"Phew!" I said, as the salesclerk handed over the bag that contained the clothes I'd been wearing when I walked in. (Claud had insisted that I wear my new outfit, so I could learn to feel at home in it.) "We're all set. How about a Super Burrito at Casa Grande? I'll treat."

Claudia was looking at me as if she thought I'd lost my mind. "All set?" she asked. "Have you forgotten about makeup? And shoes? We still have a lot to do."

I groaned. "Makeup? I have to wear makeup?"

"Just try it. They have a great counter here where they'll make you up for free."

I could see she wasn't going to buckle, so I agreed — on the condition that my reward would be a Super Burrito. I then spent the next ten minutes seated on an uncomfortable stool with my eyes closed while a woman named Lana applied about three pounds of cream, foundation, powder, blush, and mascara to my face. I kept telling her I wanted a natural look, and she kept agreeing. Then she'd add another product to the list of essential items I was going to have to buy and use.

It was a nightmare.

And when I opened my eyes, the nightmare didn't end. I looked at myself in the mirror Lana held up and saw a thirty-five-year-old woman who looked as if she should be reporting the seven o'clock news. "You can wash it off, you can wash it off," I told myself. It was the only way to keep from screaming.

Next was a quick journey to the land of Antoinette's Shoe Tree, where Claudia made me try on not just one, but *five* pairs of shoes before she found a pair she approved of. They were black strappy things with a chunky heel, and all I can say is they won't be replacing my running shoes as daily footwear.

Finally, the torture was over. I got my Super Burrito — though by then I'd nearly lost my appetite — and we met Charlie for the ride home. I glared at him so hard when we first saw him that he didn't say a thing, but I could see it was nearly killing him to keep his mouth shut.

Then there was the BSC meeting to sit through, where I had to listen to all my friends tell me how wonderful I looked while Claudia sat nearby gloating. I couldn't wait to go home, take off the shoes, scrub my face, and trade the skirt and blouse for a pair of sweats and a T-shirt (one that had cost four ninety-nine, that is). Still, before I did all that, I couldn't help taking one look at the new me. And you know what? Even though the makeup was overdone and the shoes were too shiny, the outfit really did look pretty good. I could tell that with a few changes here and a little adjustment there I would be able to wear it comfortably on my (ugh! eek!) blind date. I had to give Claudia some credit. She really is a good shopper.

But I'll never, *never* understand why she thinks it's fun.

CHAPTER 8

Thursday

Yahoo! I'm proud to report that the kids had a real breakthrough today, with just a tiny bit of help from the BSC. By the time I left the Kormans', things were looking up for the All-Kids Dance. (But believe me, it was a different story when I first arrived....)

Abby was feeling pretty pleased with herself. I could see it in her notebook entry, and I heard it in her voice when she called on Thursday night to fill me in on her afternoon sitting job. I was happy too, since everyone in the BSC had played a part in helping the kids work things out.

Mrs. Korman had asked Abby to arrive at three-thirty that afternoon. A blast of noise greeted her as she entered the house — a meeting of the SAKDC (Stoneybrook All-Kids Dance Committee, naturally) was in full swing.

"It sounded more like a riot than a meeting," Abby told me later. "There was shouting, there was yelling, things were being thrown — " she laughed. "I couldn't blame Mrs. Korman for wanting me there to help."

The cast of characters was the same: Tiffany and Maria, Linny and Hannie and Karen. The Pike triplets had arrived and so had Charlotte and Becca. For a second Abby thought about calling for another sitter: After all, she had ten kids on her hands. But then she decided she didn't need to, with Mrs. Korman around. The older kids could help out with the younger ones, if necessary. And in any case, this was a meeting, not a play group.

Abby stuck two fingers in her mouth and

whistled loudly. "Yo!" she called. The kids stopped their squabbling and looked up.

"Yo, what?" asked Jordan Pike.

Abby saw Maria and Tiffany giggle, as if Jordan had made an extremely witty joke. Then they stopped laughing and glared at each other. Abby wondered what *that* was about but didn't stop to ask.

"Yo, you!" said Abby. "All of you. What's the racket about? I thought this was a meeting."

"It is," said Tiffany. "At least it's supposed to be. If some people would just stick to the subcommittees they've been assigned to, maybe we could accomplish something." She gave her sister another dirty look.

"I can't help it," said Maria. "I just decided that the food committee needed me more than the music committee."

"We do need her," said Jordan. "She's the only one who knows the recipe for Rice Krispies Treats."

Tiffany sighed. "Anyway," she said, "that's not the only problem. We just have so much to do, and we haven't even made a final decision on a theme."

"Yes we have," said Adam. "The theme is The Big Gross-out."

"Yea!" yelled his brothers. Then all three Pike triplets started talking at once.

"We're going to have eyeballs everywhere, and fake blood poured all around," said Byron happily.

"And fake boogers," added Adam. "Don't forget the fake boogers."

"And brains and severed hands and — " Jordan began.

Several of the other kids started yelling at the same time, and Abby had to whistle once again. "Whoa," she said. "I can't hear you, Linny. What did you say?"

"I said that we didn't all agree on the gross-out theme," said Linny in a softer voice. "I still want the *Star Trek* theme, and so does Charlotte."

Charlotte nodded, crossing her arms. "That's right," she said. "That's what I voted for." She flashed a grateful smile at Linny, who blushed.

"Wait! What about the Autumn Leaves idea?" asked Becca. "I thought *that* was what we'd agreed on."

"Right," said Melody. "That's what I thought."

"No, no!" shouted Karen. "You're all wrong. We're having a Sixties theme. You know, tie-dye and everything." She turned to Bill. "Aren't we?" she asked.

"Don't ask me," he said, shrugging. "I thought we were doing a Tropical Island thing."

Abby could see that the group was no further along with their decision making than they had been during the meeting I'd attended. "It sounds as if you all need to talk a little more," she suggested. "I mean, the subcommittees can't really start doing any work until the theme is decided, right?"

Tiffany agreed reluctantly. "I'm starting to see why Shannon's temper is so short lately," she told Abby. "Planning a dance sure is hard work."

The kids settled down to a more reasonable discussion, and Abby sat back and observed. "That was when I figured out what was really going on," she told me. "It became obvious as I watched. The kids were only arguing about the theme as a way to avoid their *real* concern."

Which was?

Who was going to take whom to the dance. Abby saw that the kids were worried. It was clear to her that Charlotte was hoping to go with Linny, but that Linny was probably too shy to ask her. Bill was paying lots of attention to Hannie. And both Tiffany and Maria were gaga over Jordan, who couldn't seem less interested in either of them.

How did Abby know all this? It was the little things, she told me later. The way Linny turned beet-red every time Charlotte said anything to him. And the way Bill kept socking Hannie in the arm ("a true sign of love in the nine-year-old," said Abby). And she couldn't miss the way Tiffany and Maria jockeyed for position with Jordan, each of them doing their best to attract his attention.

None of this made Abby happy. The next time Mrs. Korman came in to check on things, Abby decided to slip away and make a few calls — to me and to other BSC members — to ask our advice on what to do. "Those kids are too young to be worrying about dates," she told me. "The dance is going to be a disaster, and there are going to be a lot of hurt feelings unless we do something about this. But what?"

She talked to me, to Claudia, and to Mary Anne. We considered the options and came up with the only answer that seemed right. Then Abby went back to the room where the kids were meeting.

"Listen, everybody," she said. "I think we have a problem here that needs to be taken care of. This is a dance we're planning, right? And everybody wants to have a good time. But you know what? Having a good time is something you can do on your own. Just because it's a dance doesn't mean you have to pair up."

Linny looked visibly relieved. "You mean we don't have to have dates to go to the dance?" he asked. "But I thought — "

"I know," said Abby gently. "You thought

because older kids take dates to dances, you have to too."

"But we don't?" asked Melody shyly.

"No, you don't," said Abby. "In fact, the other baby-sitters and I have come to a decision. We know it's your dance, but we want to make one rule. And that rule is, no dating. This is going to be a no-date dance."

"Yes!" cried Adam. Then he looked embarrassed. "I mean," he said, trying to sound a little more mature, "I think that's a very good idea. Especially because girls have cooties," he added under his breath.

The other kids quickly agreed to the rule. Abby noticed that Maria and Tiffany, while seemingly a little disappointed by the news, smiled at each other and gave up their competition for Jordan's attention. Instead, they turned to working out the details of the dance, and so did the other kids. With the tension gone, it didn't take them long to agree on a theme — the Tropical Island idea won out — and to break down into committees again for some serious work. Satisfied, Abby sat back and let the SAKDC roll. She'd done her part; now they could do the rest.

CHAPTER 9

I'd like to say it started out well.

I'd like to say Steve turned out to be the perfect boy for me.

I'd like to say it wasn't the worst date in the history of the universe.

But I can't, because it didn't, and he isn't, and it was.

Think I'm exaggerating? Well, wait until I tell the whole story.

It all began after the BSC meeting on Friday night. I'd brought my new outfit over to Claudia's house so we could dress together. She insisted on doing my makeup, and she was so excited about the date that she just babbled away. "Mark and I know that you and Steve are going to hit it off. Mark says all the girls at Kelsey are after Steve," she added as she puffed on some powder that made me itch and sneeze. "You look awesome," she finally said as she added the last touches of lip gloss.

"Steve is going to flip when he sees you."

I opened my eyes and looked at myself in the mirror. I still wasn't used to the sight of myself wearing makeup. If Steve flipped for the person he was meeting, I thought, he wouldn't be flipping for the real Kristy Thomas. But it wasn't worth arguing about with Claudia. So I just smiled and thanked her. Then I put on my new clothes and sat there feeling uncomfortable and stiff, waiting for Claudia to put together one of her creative outfits.

It was fun to watch as she pulled practically every piece of clothing she owns out of her closet and drawers. (Her bed was about three feet deep in discards by the time she finished.) She'd put on a skirt and then try on five or six sweaters, blouses, and T-shirts with it. Then she'd toss the skirt aside and try a dress. Or overalls, which she then had to pair with each of the tops all over again. She probably tried on more outfits in that half hour than I've tried on in my life. Finally, she settled on a pink corduroy miniskirt with a lime green sweater. I know it sounds yucky, but on her it looked terrific. She pulled her hair up into a ponytail, wrapped a lime green scrunchie around it, and spiked out her bangs with gel. Then she did her makeup in about fifteen seconds — I guess she has that routine down to a science — and flopped down on the bed next to me, ready to go.

Mark and Steve were supposed to pick us up at six forty-five. By seven, they still hadn't arrived. I didn't mind much. In fact, I thought I'd be happiest if they didn't show up at all. Claudia pretended she didn't mind either, but I had a feeling this wasn't the first time Mark had been late for a date. When the doorbell finally rang, it was ten after seven.

"Claudia!" called Mrs. Kishi from downstairs. "Your friends are here."

"Coming," Claud called back. Then she looked at me and smiled. "Ready?" she asked. "You look great. Let's just have fun, okay?"

"Okay," I said, smiling back. I had to admit it was a little exciting to think about the boy waiting downstairs. Maybe he really was the right guy for me. Maybe I'd fall in love at first sight.

Right. And maybe I'll learn how to fly tomorrow.

I hate to admit that Claudia was right, but you know what? First impressions really can tell you a lot. Within five minutes of meeting Steve, I knew he was not Mr. Right. He wasn't even Mr. Okay-for-the-Time-Being. But, being the gracious and open-minded person I am, I stuck with the date and even tried my best to have a good time.

But let me back up to my first glimpse of Steve. Claudia and I came down the stairs to find Mark and Steve sitting uncomfortably on the sofa, making small talk with Mr. and Mrs. Kishi. Both of them jumped up the second they saw us. "Hey, you look terrific," Mark said to Claudia, smiling at her. I didn't hear him apologize for being late, which bothered me a little. But Claudia just smiled back.

"Thanks," she said. "Mark, this is Kristy Thomas."

"Hey," Mark said to me. "Kristy, this is Steve."

"Hi, Steve," I said. He was cute. There was no denying that fact. He was tall and had deep blue eyes and brown hair that flopped perfectly over his forehead. But his clothes! He was wearing a Dallas Cowboys cap, a blue satin Yankees warm-up jacket (the kind that costs a *lot*), jeans, and a Chicago Bulls T-shirt. He looked like a walking advertisement for the NFL, the AL, and the NBA. (That's the National Football League, the American League, and the National Basketball Association, for those of you who are sports impaired.)

"Hey," he said, and I could tell he was looking me over too. He seemed to approve, because I saw him glance at Mark and nod. I felt as if I'd been rated.

"Well, we'd better be on our way," said

Mark, "if we want to make it to the movie. My brother's waiting outside in the car."

"Have fun, girls," said Mrs. Kishi. "And Claudia, don't forget to be home by ten-thirty." She walked us to the door and waved as we headed down the front walk.

We climbed into Mark's brother's car. Fortunately, Claudia sat in the middle of the backseat, between Steve and me. (Mark sat up front.) I think I would have been too nervous sitting next to Steve. Nobody talked much until we reached Pizza Express, where we'd planned to eat dinner.

We claimed a booth — the place was packed — and sat down, Steve and me on one side and Mark and Claudia on the other. Still nobody said much. Then a waitress brought menus and somehow deciding on pizza toppings broke the ice. It's always fun to find out who likes what on their pizza.

We agreed on mushrooms and pepperoni, and we put in our order. Then there was another awkward pause in the conversation. I decided to try to move things along.

"So I hear you like sports, Steve," I said. (As if I couldn't have told by his outfit.)

"Oh, sure, I'm totally into sports."

"Great," I said. "I am too."

"Cool. What do you collect?"

"Collect? I — "

"I collect mostly baseball stuff," he interrupted. "You know, cards that are worth a lot, autographs, things like that. But I like basketball stuff too. I'm especially interested in things that gain in value over the years. I have this one baseball card that my father says will send my kids through college someday." He laughed, and Mark joined in. Claudia and I just looked at each other.

This guy wasn't into sports. At least not the way I am. My idea of being a sports fan is standing out on the field with my favorite old baseball glove, waiting for one of the Krushers to hit a fly ball toward me so I can teach the rest of the team how to catch it. I had a feeling Steve wouldn't know a fly ball if it smacked into his nose — unless Mickey Mantle's autograph was on it, in which case he'd probably contact a card dealer immediately.

Still, I wanted to give him a chance. Just because he was more interested in sports collectibles than in playing sports didn't mean he wasn't a nice guy. I tried again. "Who's your favorite athlete?" I asked.

"Depends. Whoever's the hottest at the moment. That means their autograph is worth the most."

My mouth dropped open. This was unbelievable. How could Steve call himself a sports fan? "Don't you care about — " I began, forgetting for the moment that I was supposed to be making a good first impression. I was about to go into a speech about what it means to be an athlete, and how it isn't about money. I saw Claudia shoot me a warning glance, but I ignored her. What I couldn't ignore, though, was the pizza. It arrived at that moment, steaming hot and giving off the most delicious smell. I forgot my speech and helped myself to a slice.

Nobody said anything for awhile. We were too busy eating. Then, when we'd each finished our first slice, we started talking again. Only this time Mark and Steve did most of the talking — to each other. They talked about how this boy in Steve's school had made the world's largest spitball, and how Mark's brother had customized his car. They totally ignored Claudia and me.

I did not like Steve, and frankly, I didn't think Mark was all that great either. I wanted to like Mark, I really did. And I could see why Claudia liked him. He could be sweet, for instance, when he told her how nice she looked, or when he offered her the best piece of pepperoni from his pizza. But I thought she could do much, much better. I didn't like that he'd been late for our date, and I didn't appreciate the way he was ignoring Claudia. He and Steve both seemed more interested in each other than in us. Maybe they didn't know how to talk to girls, but at least they could make an effort. Steve hadn't asked me one question about myself.

I looked at Claudia and forced a smile. No way could I tell her that Mark wasn't good enough for her. She liked him, and that's what mattered. To be a good friend, I'd have to try my best to like him too. Claudia smiled back at me. For all I could tell, she was having a good time.

Soon the pizza was nearly gone. The jukebox had been cranked up, and Mark and Steve were jamming along with every song, doing their best air guitar acts. Finally, Claudia checked her watch. "Hey, we're going to miss the beginning of the movie if we don't move it," she said.

We split the check four ways. I don't believe in letting guys pay for everything, especially since I earn plenty of money baby-sitting. Then we headed down the street to the Stoneybrook Cinema, the boys walking together in front of Claudia and me.

"He's cute," Claudia whispered to me. "Don't you think?"

"Sure," I said. "He's cute." I knew Claudia wanted me to like Steve, but this wasn't the time to tell her what I thought.

"It's fun to double-date with you," said Claudia. "Just think, we could do all kinds of things together."

I didn't answer. I couldn't think of anything to say. Luckily, we arrived at the cinema, where we lined up to pay for tickets. Claudia and I were both dying to see *Paris for Two*, a comedy. I stepped up to the window next to Steve, just in time to hear him say, "Two for *Death Zone*." He turned to me with a smile. "The movie's my treat."

What could I say? From everything I'd heard, *Death Zone* is a bloody action movie with loud music and plenty of fight scenes, exactly the kind of movie I hate.

Did I sit through it? You bet. Was I sorry? Yup. Most of the time I thought about other things, trying to ignore the gore on the screen.

Afterward, during the ride home in Mark's brother's car, Steve brought up the All-Stoneybrook Dance. "So, is it a date?" he asked.

I was flabbergasted. Why on earth would he want to go out with me again? We had nothing in common, and he'd barely talked to me all night. But I couldn't think of a nice way to say, "Not in a million years," so I just told him I'd let him know. I'd figure out how to say no later.

CHAPTER 10

History books of the future will probably show that it was the Spaghetti Incident that ended the Sister War. Some experts might argue with that and push the idea that the Bucket Episode was more influential, but they are in the minority. There are even those who will claim that the Sweater Situation was the turning point, but most people know that's ridiculous.

I, myself, think it can't be explained so easily. The Sister War was a complex chain of events, and only those who were there will ever really understand it. Of course, I could give myself credit for arranging the final cease-fire, but I doubt I'll ever receive the recognition I deserve for my role in bringing peace.

But seriously . . . By the time I sat for Tiffany and Maria on Monday afternoon, the Sister War had hit its peak. And Tiffany and Maria weren't kidding around anymore with baby pranks such as lost phone messages. They'd moved on to the big stuff. Plus, they'd started to have their own competition — over Jordan Pike — which only complicated things. They'd work together for the sake of aggravating Shannon, but then the second they'd got a reaction from her they would squabble again. They weren't arguing anymore about which of them would go to the dance with Jordan, since dates had been ruled out, but they still found plenty to quarrel about, for instance, which of them would wear a certain red sweater they both liked (which happened to belong to Shannon, though that was beside the point), or who would ask Jordan to dance first.

That's what they were arguing about after school on Monday. It was another of those perfect fall days when the air is crisp but the sun warms you. We decided to enjoy the weather and take a walk.

"Kristy, don't you think I have the right to ask Jordan first, since I'm older?" asked Tiffany.

"I don't know what that has to do with it," said Maria. "I think I should have the first chance because — " she thought for a second, unable to come up with a good reason. "Just because, that's why," she said finally, crossing her arms and nodding.

I held up my hands. "Don't put me in the middle of this," I said. "You'll have to work it out for yourselves. But I don't think you should be so concerned about who dances with whom. Just have a good time! That's what dances are for."

"Oh, I'll have a good time, all right," said Tiffany, "as long as I dance with Jordan." She pretended to swoon. "He's so, so cute."

I knew that she and Maria were just fooling around with the idea of having a crush on a boy. After all, they were too young to be interested in dating. Still, I thought they'd be better off if they forgot about the subject.

"How are things at home?" I asked. When I saw Maria's frown and Tiffany's grimace, I almost wished I had kept my question to myself.

"Shannon's avoiding us," said Maria.

"It's like we're invisible," agreed Tiffany. "Unless she wants to yell at us for something, that is," she added almost under her breath.

"Why would she be yelling at you?" I asked. "You aren't still pulling pranks, are you?" (Oh, I was so innocent.)

"Well," said Maria.

"Um," said Tiffany.

"Guys?" I asked.

Tiffany bent down to pick up a pinecone. "I guess we've done a couple of things," she mumbled. "But she deserves it!" she added, straightening up. "It's a Sister War, remember?"

"That's right," said Maria, nodding. "We wouldn't do those things to her if she just spent some time with us, like a good big sister should."

They sounded as if they were trying to convince themselves. "So, what have you done to her?" I asked casually.

"Nothing that bad," said Maria. "Well, except for the business with the sweater."

"The bucket thing was kind of mean too," said Tiffany, reflecting. "But the one that really made her mad was the hair dye."

"Hair dye?" I asked, arching an eyebrow. "I want to hear about the other things too, but why don't you start with that one?"

This time it was Maria who bent down, to pick up a stick. I think she was avoiding my eyes. So Tiffany started to talk.

"Well, it was just that we emptied out part of her shampoo," she said, "and then we filled up the bottle with — "

"With hair dye?" I asked. "Oh my lord. What color?"

"Sort of purple," admitted Tiffany.

"What do you mean *sort* of purple?" I asked. "There's purple and there's not-purple. Which was it?"

"It was *mega*-purple!" shouted Maria, tossing away her stick. She couldn't help grinning. "She looked like Barney."

"But it was the kind that washes right out," put in Tiffany quickly. "We were careful about that."

"I'm sure Shannon appreciated your thoughtfulness," I said.

Maria shook her head. "Nope," she said seriously. "She went bananas. Then she washed her hair, like, nine times in a row. I think she ran out of hot water on about the sixth shampoo, but she kept doing it until all the purple was out."

"Her hair looked kind of like straw after that," said Tiffany, remembering. "And Mom was miffed because she'd used up all the towels."

"I can imagine," I said. We were walking by a low stone wall. I sat down on it — the stones were warm from the sun — and patted the spots on either side of me. "Now that you've told me about the dye incident, why don't you fill me in on the other things you've done to Shannon?"

Tiffany sat on my right, Maria on my left. Maria pretended to brush some dust off her jacket sleeve while Tiffany acted fascinated with the surface of the stone wall.

"Come on, let's hear it," I said. "It can't be that bad."

"It isn't!" said Maria. "But Shannon acts like we're criminals or something."

"She'd probably be happy if we were thrown into jail," agreed Tiffany. "But it's not as if we've done anything really illegal."

"Ahem," I said. "Why don't you let me be the judge of that? Start with the sweater."

"Well, we were just trying to be helpful," said Maria. "You know how we are." She looked up at me through her eyelashes, all innocence.

"So we did some laundry for her," added Tiffany. "How were we supposed to know that wool shrinks?"

"She has this brand-new white sweater," said Maria. "It looked really good on her, but now it won't even fit my old Cabbage Patch doll."

"I thought you were supposed to wash everything in really hot water," explained Tiffany, "if you want it to be clean."

"At least, that's what you told Shannon," I said. "I have a feeling you might have known just a little more about it than that. Besides, anyone can read the label in a sweater — or the directions on the detergent box. Doing laundry is not rocket science."

Tiffany looked down at her hands. Maria stared off at a lamppost.

"So what?" asked Tiffany finally. "I mean, even so, it was only a sweater. Shannon made, like, a federal case out of it."

"She made us take an oath swearing we'd never touch any of her clothes ever again," said Maria.

"Hmm," I said. "And you did?"

"Of course," said Tiffany. "We had no choice."

"Yet you're arguing over who's going to wear her red sweater," I said. "It doesn't sound as if you take your oath too seriously."

"I had my fingers crossed," admitted Maria.

Tiffany held up one foot. "Toes," she said. She giggled a little, but I shot her a Look and she stopped.

The girls were having just a little too much fun with the Sister War, I thought. Even though they were making Shannon angrier and angrier, it seemed as if they were swept up in the pleasure of torturing her. Yet all they wanted, more than anything, was her attention. I knew there had to be a better way. Meanwhile, I still had to find out one more thing. "Okay," I said. "Let's have the whole story. What did you do with that bucket?"

"Bucket?" repeated Maria.

"What bucket?" asked Tiffany.

"Guys," I said warningly.

"I read about it in a book," said Tiffany. "It's one of the oldest practical jokes in the world."

"You didn't — " I began.

"We did," said Tiffany. "We balanced a

bucket on top of her door so when she opened it — well, you know the rest."

"Except we made the trick even better," said Maria, kicking her heels against the stone wall happily. "We didn't put water in the bucket. That would have been too boring."

"Right," I said. "Really boring. And Shannon would hate that. So what did you fill the bucket with?"

Tiffany giggled. "I'll give you a hint. It was red. And wiggly."

"That's two hints!" cried Maria. "I want to give one too. It had to be in the refrigerator for awhile first."

I couldn't believe my ears. "Not Jell-O!" I said. "You must be kidding."

"Nope," said Maria. "Not kidding."

"So Shannon ended up covered in cherry Jell-O?" I asked, seeing the awful picture in my mind's eye.

"Raspberry, actually," said Tiffany with a touch of pride.

"Hoo, boy. No wonder Shannon's trying to avoid you two." I glanced at my watch. "Speaking of Shannon, she's probably home by now and wondering where we are. We better go." The three of us headed home without talking much more. I was trying hard to figure out a way to convince the girls to give up the Sister

War. They were probably busy plotting their next prank.

Shannon's backpack was on the kitchen table when we returned to the Kilbournes', but she — and Astrid — were nowhere in sight. "They must have gone for a walk," I said. "Well, how about if you guys start in on your homework while I'm here to help?"

The girls agreed, so we trooped upstairs. They changed, then sat down at their desks to work. I helped Tiffany with some math first, then went into Maria's room to help her with spelling. I thought I heard Tiffany slip downstairs while I was helping Maria, and I knew that Maria had gone to the kitchen earlier. I figured they were helping themselves to snacks.

After half an hour, I heard the front door slam, and Astrid came bounding up the stairs to look for Tiffany and Maria. But Shannon didn't follow her. I was just about to head downstairs to say hi to her when I heard a bloodcurdling scream from the kitchen.

CHAPTER 11

I ran to the door of Maria's room and looked out into the hall. "What was *that*?" I cried. "Tiffany, are you okay?"

Tiffany poked her head out of her room. "I'm fine," she said. "Who yelled?"

I heard a stifled giggle behind me and turned to see Maria with her hand over her mouth. "Take a guess," she told her sister. Tiffany started to giggle too.

"What have you two been up to?" I asked, putting my hands on my hips. "This isn't funny anymore. That scream sounded serious." I raised my voice. "Shannon, are you okay?"

There was no answer.

"Shannon?" I called, a little louder.

Then I saw her. She'd appeared at the bottom of the stairs.

She did not look happy.

In one hand she held her backpack, the one I'd seen on the kitchen table. In the other she held a limp, knotted, slimy tangle that looked like fat white worms.

Spaghetti. Cooked spaghetti in her backpack. The girls had outdone themselves.

"Oh my lord," I said. I turned to glare at Maria and Tiffany, but they'd disappeared.

Shannon started up the stairs with a purposeful look on her face. I had a very bad feeling about what she might do or say to her sisters, if she could catch them.

"Shannon," I said, putting out a hand as if to stop her. "Wait — "

"Wait for what?" she asked. "I've just about had it with their pranks. And I'm going to tell them so."

I gulped. I knew a confrontation right now was not a good idea. Not with Shannon this angry, and the girls so pleased with themselves. The Sister War had gone far enough. If I could just help Shannon cool down a bit before she yelled at them, maybe the three of them could talk things over and make up. "Don't you think — " I began, but Shannon interrupted me.

"Whose side are you on, here, anyway?" she asked. "And, by the way, what kind of babysitter lets two little kids go around pulling pranks like this?" She held up the spaghetti and shook it in my face.

I stepped back as if she'd slapped me.

"Kristy, I'm sorry," she said. "I didn't mean that. It's not your fault that my sisters have turned into the hugest pests this side of a giant cockroach." She sat down on the stairs and, with a big sigh, put her face in her hands.

That was when she realized she was still holding the spaghetti.

"Oh, ew," she said. She glanced up at me. For a second she looked as if she were about to start crying. Instead, she began to laugh.

I joined her. Soon we were both laughing so hard we couldn't stop. My stomach hurt. Tears were rolling down my face. I had to sit down next to Shannon on the stairs. Every time I looked at her I started cracking up all over again.

Then, suddenly, she stopped laughing. She looked extremely serious. I noticed that she was looking — or, rather, glaring — at something behind me. I turned my head just in time to see Maria and Tiffany duck back into their rooms. When I looked back at Shannon, she was just starting to stand up.

"Uh, Shannon," I said quickly. "How about if we go downstairs for a cup of cocoa?"

She glanced at me. "In a minute," she said.

I touched her arm. "Let's talk first," I said pleadingly.

She glanced at me again. Then she nodded. "Okay," she said. "Let's talk."

94

She followed me downstairs, and I could almost swear I heard two loud sighs of relief behind us. I hoped Tiffany and Maria appreciated that I'd just saved their skins.

We headed into the kitchen. I filled up the kettle with water and set it to boil on the stove. When the cocoa was ready, I handed a mug to Shannon.

"Thanks," she said. She blew on the top of her cocoa to cool it, then took a sip. "Mmm, good," she said.

I'd been thinking while I was making that cocoa, and I'd made a decision. Just this once, I thought, I'd keep my mouth shut and listen.

It wasn't easy. I had to think about how to listen. Mary Anne would have been perfect at a time like this, since listening comes naturally to her.

It does not come naturally to me.

Fortunately, there was plenty to listen *to*. Once she started, Shannon had a hard time stopping. It only took one little question from me and she was off and running. All I said was, "Shannon, is everything okay?"

She bit her lip and shook her head. "Not really," she admitted. She looked down and smoothed her skirt. (She was still dressed in her school uniform.) "Not at all," she added.

I could see she was having a hard time keeping the tears from falling. "What's going on?" I asked. (Okay, so I asked two little questions.)

"I just feel so *tired* all the time," Shannon said. "And overwhelmed. I guess I've just taken on too much, but I don't know what to do about it. I mean, I *like* all the things I do. French Club, Honor Society, the school play, the dance committee — all of it. It's fun to be involved." She paused to sniff a little and wipe her eyes.

"I don't want to give anything up," she went on. "But something's not right with the way things are going."

"Not right?" I repeated.

She took another sip of cocoa and sighed. "No," she said, shaking her head. "Not right. I mean, I can't remember the last time I sat down to watch some dumb TV show, or the last time I read a book just for enjoyment."

"Sounds like you don't have much time to relax," I said.

"Exactly," she agreed. "No time at all. And, as I'm sure you've noticed," she gave me a rueful look, "I haven't had time to be a BSC member lately, much less take on any jobs. I miss sitting." She paused for a second. "Hey, do we have any graham crackers? I'm hungry all of a sudden."

"Not only do you have graham crackers," I said, jumping up from my seat, "you have chocolate-covered graham crackers." I opened a cupboard, took out a box, and plunked it down in front of Shannon. "Funny how I know the contents of your family's cabinets better than you do."

"Funny, but not so funny either. It's not just the cabinets you know better."

"What do you mean?"

Shannon frowned. "Tiffany and Maria," she said. "I think you have a better idea of what's going on with them than I do."

"Well . . ." I began, not knowing what to say. "Tell me what *you* think is going on."

"I have no idea," said Shannon. "All I know is that they're driving me nuts. Normally I'd say I miss spending time with them, but these days I'm not so sure. They've been such pains lately. Why would I want to be around them? I just don't understand why they're pulling all these pranks on me, especially now, when the last thing I need is any more complications in my life." She looked over at me. "Maybe you can explain."

Finally! She was asking my opinion. Or at least she was asking me to talk. That I could do.

"I know it seems as if they're out to make you crazy," I began carefully. "But I'm not so sure that's their motivation."

"What do you mean?"

"Remember in third grade when some kid

would be acting all obnoxious in class?" I asked. "And your teacher would say, 'Johnny just wants attention'?"

Shannon nodded. "I always thought that was pretty strange," she said. "Like, the teacher would tell us to ignore him. Well, if he was doing that stuff for attention, how was ignoring him going to help?"

I made one last monumental effort and didn't say a thing.

After a few seconds, a light went on in Shannon's eyes. "Ohhh!" she said. "You mean they're doing it for attention?"

I nodded. "I think maybe they are," I said. "I think they miss you."

"That's ridiculous! I'm right here." Then she thought for a second. "Oh. Maybe I'm not. I guess that's what I've just been saying." She was quiet for a little while, and I could practically see the wheels turning in her mind.

We finished our cocoa in silence while Shannon thought everything over. I had a definite feeling that the Sister War would not last much longer. (Note to Nobel Peace Prize Committee: That's Kristy Thomas, T-H-O-M-A-S, and I can be reached at 1210 McLelland Road, Stoneybrook, CT 06800.)

CHAPTER 12

"Welcome to the madhouse!" Alan Gray swooped past us as he zigzagged through the crowd.

For once, he wasn't exaggerating. The place was in total chaos, no matter which way I looked.

What place? The Stoneybrook Community Center. And why was I there? Good question. I was asking myself the same thing. But the fact was, I was there with my friends — we'd come directly from Wednesday's BSC meeting — to help put the finishing touches on plans for the All-Stoneybrook Dance, which would take place in three short days. We were a little late, but I was hoping we'd still be able to help out.

The committee had chosen the community center for several reasons. First, it has a huge gym; all the community basketball leagues play there. Second, it's conveniently located. And third, it was neutral ground. I could see that trying to plan a dance that would please kids from three very different schools was — well, let's just say it wasn't easy.

The plan for Wednesday was for the committee plus any interested kids from each school to meet at the community center and work out the final details of the dance. Also, we hoped to do most of the decorating, so that only the finishing touches would have to be added on Saturday afternoon.

That was the idea anyway.

So far, it didn't look as if a thing had been done. And, at the rate things were going, it would be a major victory if even one strand of crepe paper ended up being hung. From what I could tell, there was one word missing from the vocabulary lists at each of the three schools.

That word? Cooperation.

Now, supposedly, the committee had already worked out the details of the dance. Decisions — about music, about decorations, about food — had been made by representatives from each school. All that was left to do was carry out those decisions. At least, that's what I thought. Unfortunately, nobody else seemed to agree. Instead, most of the kids in the community center that night thought that all the plans for the dance were open to debate.

In every corner of the gym, small groups of kids were arguing about — well, about every possible thing you could imagine. And most of the BSC members jumped right in. Me? Frankly, I didn't care that much about the details of the dance. I'd just come to help out. I decided to cruise around and see what was going on.

"Berry punch? That sounds absolutely vomitacious." Greer Carson, one of Shannon's friends from SDS, was talking to a group of kids that included Shannon, Stacey, and Mary Anne, as well as two guys from Kelsey. I recognized one of them, Al Hall, but I didn't know the other.

"We always have berry punch at our dances," said Mary Anne, looking a little hurt. "I don't see what's wrong with it."

"But the committee decided on lemonade," said Al.

"Lemonade?" Greer rolled her eyes. "I'd rather die of thirst."

"Well, what did *you* have in mind?" asked the guy from Kelsey.

"I don't know," said Greer impatiently. "Something sophisticated. Something interesting. Something out of the ordinary."

"How about if we just have something *easy*?" asked Stacey. "I mean, wouldn't it be simplest to go with the committee's recommendation? After all, they already put a lot of thought into the refreshments."

Good for Stacey, I thought. The voice of reason speaks again.

Unfortunately, nobody listened to the voice of reason.

I shrugged and strolled over to another spot, below one of the basketball hoops. The group there was discussing decorations. I spotted Claudia (in the thick of that discussion, naturally) and Mal and an SDS guy named Kevin, who's friends with Bart, and a girl named Polly, who looked as if she might be Kevin's girlfriend. Two girls from Kelsey, Amanda Kerner and Jacqueline Vecchio, were also there.

"How in the world could anyone think purple and orange are a good color combination?" Claudia was asking as I arrived. She held a roll of crepe paper in each hand, and she was looking down at them disgustedly.

"Actually, a majority of the committee agreed on those colors," said Polly with a sniff. "I was one of the ones who voted for them."

"Oh." Claudia looked embarrassed for just a second. Then she launched in again. "And why can't we do something a little more creative than just stringing crepe paper around the place? Why not build a stage set, or paint a mural?"

"We only have two more days," Kevin reminded her. "And anyway, I think the committee had some pretty creative ideas."

"You call purple tablecloths creative?" asked Claudia.

"Don't forget the centerpieces," said Amanda. "The ones Kelsey's donating from our last dance."

"I saw those," said Polly. "And they're very nice. But I don't think the yellow and red color scheme really works with — "

"We could make new centerpieces," Mal interrupted eagerly. "I just learned this neat way to make flowers out of plain old tissues. It's really easy, and — "

"Tissue paper flowers are *so* last week," Claudia broke in. "I know I could come up with something great if you'd just let me think for a minute." She was so caught up in her urge to be creative that she didn't even notice the hurt look on Mal's face.

I moved on. One more group sat sprawled across a section of bleachers, arguing vehemently about music.

"No way am I going to dance to even one Beatles song," I heard Pete Black say. "I vote for the stuff you can really thrash to. You know, like head-banging tunes."

"I *love* the Beatles," said Cokie Mason, putting her hands on her hips. "How dare you say anything against them!"

Personally? I'd be the first one to say nasty things about the Beatles — if I knew it would make Cokie mad. And I adore the Beatles. I just don't adore Cokie. She's the biggest pain at SMS.

I saw Jessi, who was sitting next to her, shaking her head, and I knew she agreed with me.

"How about some Beatles *and* some metal?" asked Emily Bernstein, who's also from SMS. She's very levelheaded, and it was just like her to try to make peace.

"I don't even know why you're all arguing," said a guy named Karl Schmauder. He goes to Kelsey. "The committee already made some tapes, and they're ready to go." He held up three cassettes.

"Let me see those," said Lindsey, one of Shannon's friends from SDS. She snatched the tapes. "If there's any Grateful Dead on here, any at all, I'm not going *near* this dance. I can't stand them."

Abby, sitting next to Jessi, cracked up. "You'd miss this whole dance because of one Grateful Dead song?" she asked.

"Absolutely," said Lindsey, reading through the labels on the cassettes. "You wouldn't want me to hurl all over the dance floor, would you?"

Oh man. I shook my head.

What's a dance supposed to be?

Fun.

And everyone had forgotten about fun. I had to do something to remind them.

I ran to the sound system, which Alan Gray had been busily setting up. Next to the tape player was a pile of cassettes. I rummaged through them. "Hey!" said Alan.

I waved him away. "Hold on, hold on," I muttered as I flipped through the tapes. Finally I found the perfect one. It was the newest Happy Dogs album, and it included their hit single, "I Feel Like Dancing." "Put this on," I said, shoving it toward Alan. "And make sure the sound is way up."

"Yes, your Kristiness," he said, bowing deeply.

He put in the tape and cranked up the volume. I heard the first notes and grinned. "Yess!" I said. I grabbed Alan's hand. "Come on, let's dance."

"Me?" he asked, amazed.

"Yes, you," I said. "Now." I hauled him into the middle of the gym and started to dance. At first, I felt self-conscious. All the arguing had stopped and everyone turned to stare at us. But then I was swept up into the music, and I started to have fun. Alan was having fun too. He grinned at me and I grinned back.

About a minute into the song, something else happened. First Claudia, then Shannon, then Al Hall, then five or six other kids began to drift toward the middle of the gym. They started to dance near me and Alan.

By the end of the song, every kid in that gym

was dancing. Angry looks had been replaced by smiles. Nobody had the breath to argue. And everyone had remembered what the dance was about in the first place.

We danced for about half an hour and then went back to work. Does it surprise you to hear that everything went smoothly? Well, it did. By the end of the night, the gym was transformed. The refreshments committee was in agreement. And there were no further arguments about music.

On our way out, Claudia gave me a high five. "Good work, Kristy. This dance is going to *rule*. And the four of us are going to have an awesome time."

"Four of us?" I asked.

"You, me, Mark, and Steve."

Oops. "I guess I forgot to tell you," I said. "I was inspired by the kids and their no-date dance. I called Steve the other day and told him I was going alone."

For a second, Claudia looked disappointed. Then she cheered up. "I know he wasn't the right guy for you," she said. "But you know what? We're going to have an awesome time anyway."

I had a feeling she was right.

CHAPTER 13

I sat frozen in my chair, wishing I could pull that old "put on some music and dance" trick again. Would it work? Probably not in this situation.

What situation, you ask?

The one at the Kilbourne family dinner table.

Oh, nobody was arguing the way they had been at the community center the night before. But what they were doing was worse.

They weren't talking.

Well, that's not quite true. Mrs. Kilbourne had spoken once, to offer the broccoli around. Mr. Kilbourne had said something I probably shouldn't quote when his beeper went off two seconds after he'd sat down to eat. Shannon had said "Fine" when her mom asked how her day had been. And Maria and Tiffany had each said "Thank you" when their dad served them some pot roast.

I'd said "Thank you" too, for the same reason. Other than that I'd kept my mouth shut.

As I chased a carrot around my plate with my fork, I wondered why Tiffany and Maria had begged me to stay for dinner. It's not as if I had anything to contribute to the sparkling conversation. In fact, the only thing I wanted to say was, "Thanks for a lovely dinner, I'm going home now."

But it had seemed important to the girls that I stay. They'd begged so convincingly that I couldn't figure out how to say no. Maybe they were hoping I could wave a magic wand and make everything better with their family; I don't know.

Big surprise: The Kilbournes' chaotic life was at the root of the problem for Tiffany and Maria. Everyone was too busy. The girls had said so on that Thursday afternoon while we made cookies.

"Guess how many times Dad's beeper went off during supper last night," Maria said to me as she cracked two eggs and dumped them into a bowl. "Seven, that's how many. A world record. And every time it went off, he headed straight for the phone and talked for about fifteen minutes, even though he's always promising to cut down."

"It's not as if we were having a real family dinner anyway," said Tiffany. "Mom was at a class, and Shannon had to leave early to go over to the community center."

I felt a little guilty remembering how much fun we'd had dancing.

"And Dad was reading briefs at the dinner table anyway," added Maria.

"Briefs?" I asked. I had a vision of Mr. Kilbourne reading the label on a pair of underwear, and I couldn't help giggling to myself.

"It's some kind of lawyer thing," said Maria, shrugging. "He does it all the time. Like when he's pretending to watch a movie with us, he'll really be going over some paperwork." She sounded tired.

I poured a teaspoonful of vanilla into the eggs Maria was beating. "So, has your mom been enjoying school?" I asked cautiously.

"She *loves* it," said Tiffany. She didn't look very happy for her mom.

"She's going to go full-time next semester," added Maria glumly.

"Oh." I was sorry I'd asked.

"Then, after she graduates, she'll probably find a job," said Tiffany.

I decided to change the subject. "I haven't heard about you two pulling any new pranks on Shannon. Does that mean the Sister War is over?"

"I guess," said Tiffany.

"It's over," agreed Maria.

"She was pretty mad about that spaghetti," said Tiffany. "We figured we'd better lay low for awhile. Besides, it wasn't really working." Tiffany turned on the mixer.

Nobody spoke for a few minutes as the mixer did its work. Then Tiffany reached over to turn it off.

"Has Shannon been paying more attention to you?" I asked.

"Nope," said Tiffany. She tossed back her hair. "Not like I care anymore. I've given up on her. Now that she's in the school play, we'll *never* see her."

"Shannon's in the play?" I asked. I hadn't heard anything about that.

"She just found out," said Maria. "It's not a big role, and she doesn't even seem all that excited about it. But she's going through with it."

I was surprised Shannon hadn't told me the night before, but maybe that was because she wasn't thrilled about it. I dropped a spoonful of cookie dough onto the baking sheet. "So, when do rehearsals start?" I asked.

Silence.

"Tiffany?"

"Tomorrow night," said Tiffany glumly.

"So Shannon can't come to our dance," Maria added.

"All the other kids' parents and brothers and

sisters are going to be there," said Tiffany. "But not ours." She gave a little sniffle.

"Can't your mom come?" I asked.

Maria shook her head. "She has a meeting with some other people in her class. It's about a midterm or something." She sniffled too.

"It's a study group," Tiffany explained. "And Dad has to be in New York for a meeting."

"That's a shame," I said.

Tiffany shrugged. She was trying hard not to burst into tears.

Maria, on the other hand, started to sob. "It's the first party we ever planned by ourselves, and they aren't even going to be there to see it!" she wailed. I gave her a little squeeze and stroked her hair until her crying died down.

The baking sheet was full by that time, so I put it in the oven and set a timer. Then I pulled out another baking sheet and started to fill that one up.

"Do Shannon and your parents know how much it would mean to you if they came to the dance?" I asked after a few moments.

Tiffany and Maria looked at each other. "I don't know," said Maria.

"Shannon seemed surprised when I acted upset about her not coming," Tiffany said thoughtfully. "So maybe not."

"Well, I have an assignment for you, then," I said. "There won't be time this afternoon, since we'll have to clean up the kitchen before dinner. You can do it tonight, after dinner, and after you've finished your homework."

"What do we have to do?" asked Maria suspiciously.

"Write a letter," I answered. "Actually, two letters. One to Shannon and one to your parents. You can work together."

"What are we supposed to say?" asked Tiffany. "I mean, why are we writing them letters?"

"Why? Because you have something to say. And even though you've tried to say it, the message isn't getting through."

"What message?" asked Maria.

"The one about how much you love your sister and your parents, and how much you miss them."

Maria nodded. "I could write a whole book about that," she said.

"We'll do it," added Tiffany, "but only if you stay for dinner tonight."

"I — uh — " I began. After hearing about last night's dinner, I didn't have any special wish to be a guest at the Kilbourne table.

"Please?" asked Maria.

They worked on me while we finished the cookies and cleaned up the kitchen, and finally I gave in. For some reason they needed me there that night. How could I say no?

So that's how I ended up at the table surrounded by Kilbournes who had nothing to say to each other. That was one dinner I could have skipped. I could only hope that the letters would help. If they didn't, I had no clue about what to do next.

CHAPTER 14

Friday

I guess I surprised my sisters!
I surprised myself too, for that
matter. In fact, this whole night
was full of surprises. And, unlike
some of the surprises I've had
over the past few weeks (do the
words "spaghetti" and "backpack"
ring a bell?), the ones that took
place tonight were all good ones.

Shannon certainly surprised us — her fellow club members — that night. None of us expected her to do what she did. It was the night of the All-Kids Dance, and excitement was in the air.

During our meeting that evening, we'd had calls from just about every one of our sitting charges. Charlotte Johanssen had called about a minor hair emergency. Nicky Pike called to let us know that there was no way he was going to dance with any stinky girls. Melody Korman called to ask if we thought Nicky would dance with her. Maria and Tiffany — each on a different extension — called to ask me to determine which of them most deserved to wear Shannon's red sweater (of course I told them to leave the sweater in its drawer and wear their own clothes). And Karen called three times to make sure we remembered 1) the way to the community center, where their dance was taking place as well, 2) what time to be there, and 3) that we'd promised to serve the punch and cookies.

Just after the final call from Karen, I realized it was six o'clock, time to adjourn the meeting and hightail it over to the community center. We'd planned to arrive early and help set everything up. Some of the kids' parents would be there too. I expected to see Mr. Johanssen, Mrs. Pike, and Mrs. Korman. I definitely did not expect to see Shannon.

"Hey, what are you doing here?" I asked. Shannon was waiting on the front steps of the community center. I noticed she was wearing the red sweater. I also noticed that she looked happier than I'd seen her in a long, long time.

She grinned. "I came to help out," she said.

"But what about the play?" I was thrilled to have her there, and I was hoping it meant she'd finally "heard" Tiffany and Maria's message, but I couldn't quite believe what I was seeing.

She shrugged. "I quit. I didn't really like the director — she was kind of a space cadet — and the part they gave me wasn't very interesting. I figured I had better things to do with my time."

"Well, we can sure use your help," said Jessi. "We have a lot to do, and the kids will be here in" — she glanced at her watch — "oh, no! Twenty minutes!"

At that, all eight of us charged inside, ready to set up tables, pour punch, and put out cookies. I didn't have another second to talk to Shannon all night, but she told me later how much fun she'd had.

"You should have seen the look on Tiffany's face when she saw me," she reported. "She did this huge double take. Then she grabbed Maria by the hand and the two of them came flying across the gym to me."

"What are you doing here?" demanded Maria, echoing the question I'd asked earlier. "I thought you had a play rehearsal."

"I did," Shannon said. "But I decided the dance was more important. I wanted to be here with you guys."

Maria looked unsure. "Did you quit the play?" she asked.

Shannon nodded.

"But — " Tiffany began, "we didn't want you to — "

"Don't worry," said Shannon. She explained why she'd quit, giving the same reasons she'd given us and adding a couple more. "I realized I just had too much on my plate," she told her sisters. "Something had to give. I needed to remember to have fun — and fun definitely includes spending time with you two. I remembered that when I read your letter last night." She gathered her sisters into a big group hug.

Shannon took a step back and looked at Tiffany and Maria. "Hey, you two look great," she said. "Tiffany, I like the way you did your hair. And Maria, your outfit is awesome."

"Do you think Jordan will like it?" asked Maria.

"I think he'd be crazy not to. But remember," she warned, "ten-year-old boys are not always all that interested in dancing."

"He'll dance with me," said Tiffany confidently. "I'm an older woman."

Shannon cracked up. "We'll see. In any case, I know I want to dance with both of you. And it looks as if the music is just about to start."

By that time, the gym was starting to fill up with kids. The noise level was rising. Then, suddenly, the overheard lights were turned down and some colored ones came on, making green and blue patterns all over the gym. "Yikes! We'd better move it!" said Tiffany. Before Shannon could ask where they were going, her sisters had taken off toward a low platform that had been set up near one end of the gym. Already standing on the platform were Melody and Bill, Linny and Hannie, Karen, the Pike triplets, Charlotte, and Becca: the original planning committee for the All-Kids Dance.

"Welcome, everybody," said Tiffany, speaking into a microphone. "We hope you'll have an awesome time at the first annual Stoneybrook All-Kids Dance!"

Bill took the mike next. "There are refreshments on the tables back there," he pointed out, "and plenty of punch."

"We want you all to enjoy yourselves, so

don't be shy about asking a friend to dance!" put in Karen.

"And now," said Maria, taking her turn at the mike, "let the dance begin!"

Shannon felt her eyes fill up. She was proud of her little sisters.

Then Linny bent down and fiddled with some knobs on the sound system, and suddenly the gym was filled with music. A spotlight came on, focusing on a mirrored ball hanging from the middle of the ceiling. The ball began to spin, sending fragments of light around the gym.

"All right!" Shannon yelled, pumping an arm in the air. The dance was under way.

Or was it?

Something was wrong. Nobody was dancing. The kids were lined up along the walls, the excitement on their faces replaced by anxious looks. Shannon saw her sisters glancing nervously at the Pike boys.

"Oh, no," said Shannon to herself. (All over the gym, other BSC members were saying the same thing.) Now that she saw it happening, she wondered why she hadn't predicted it. It was dance gridlock. Everybody wanted to dance, but nobody wanted to be first. What was going to break the ice?

Suddenly, a man appeared on the platform. He bowed low in front of Maria and Tiffany.

"May I have this dance?" he asked, shouting to be heard over the booming beat.

"Daddy!" yelled Maria.

"Yea!" shouted Tiffany.

The three of them jumped off the platform and began to move to the beat, there in the middle of the floor.

Shannon watched, surprised and happy. And as she did, someone tapped her on the shoulder. She turned to see her mom beaming at her. "Hi, honey," she said.

"Mom!" Shannon threw her arms around her mother. "I'm so glad to see you guys. But what are you doing here?"

They walked out into the hallway so they could talk without shouting and still watch through the doors. Mr. Kilbourne was leading his daughters across the floor and slowly but surely the space around them was filling up with other dancers.

"Surprised?" Mrs. Kilbourne asked Shannon.

"Very. And happy."

"Me too. Dad and I were talking late last night and we realized that we've both become way too busy. Maria and Tiffany need us. They made that clear in their letter. Also, we made some decisions. It took a lot of thought to figure it all out, but Dad decided to quit Rotary, which will free him up quite a bit. And I decided that I'll only sign up for two classes next semester, and I'll make sure they're at times when the girls are in school."

"That sounds great," said Shannon.

Mrs. Kilbourne nodded. "Our goal is for the family to have dinner together every night. I know that won't happen right away, but we'll work toward it."

Shannon smiled. She knew the Kilbourne family would always be busy because that was the Kilbourne way. But she felt sure that Tiffany and Maria would begin to get the attention they deserved. And, hopefully, they'd never start another Sister War! She glanced through the door and saw that the first song was ending. Mr. Kilbourne was hugging his two youngest daughters, both of whom were smiling from ear to ear.

"Let's dance!" said Shannon, pulling her mom back into the gym. Another song had just come on, and the floor was filling up with kids. Shannon and her mom headed to the spot where Mr. Kilbourne was dancing with Maria and Tiffany, and their family danced together.

The All-Kids Dance was a huge success, and not just for the Kilbourne family. Once the kids got over their shyness, they danced the night away — in groups, in pairs, and even by themselves. Nicky Pike actually danced with a few girls, Melody included. And Linny and Charlotte danced at least four dances together.

121

As for the competition between Tiffany and Maria over Jordan Pike — well, even that had a happy ending. At one point, Shannon looked around and saw Maria dancing with Adam. Then she turned the other way and saw Tiffany dancing with Byron!

It turned out to be a case of mistaken identities. Neither of the girls had a crush on Jordan. Maria found out that Adam was the boy for her, and Tiffany discovered that Byron was the boy for *her*. And Jordan? He was just as happy to dance all night with Becca Ramsey.

CHAPTER 15

The punch and cookies were laid out on the tables. The lights were down and the music was loud. The mirrored ball was spinning, sending those tiny fragments of light around the gym. The dance had begun.

It was Saturday night, and so far it looked like a replay of the night before. "I think I'm having déjà vu," I told Claudia.

"Major *who*?" Claud yelled into my ear.

"Never mind," I said, shaking my head. It was too hard to talk over the thumping beat of the music. Instead, I turned to the person on my left — Shannon — and grinned. She grinned back and nodded her head to show she agreed.

Agreed with what?

With the fact that the middle-school kids in Stoneybrook are not a whole lot more mature than the elementary school ones. (There are even some, like Alan Gray, who are *less* mature.)

In other words, nobody was dancing. The girls were lined up on one side of the gym, and the boys were on the other. On both sides, kids were jostling each other, whispering (or yelling, more likely) into each other's ears, and shooting shy glances across the room. Even the kids who had come in pairs had separated when they walked into the gym, as if there were some unspoken word about girls having to stick with girls and boys with boys.

Ugh.

I, for one, was there to have a good time. I didn't intend to stand around all night waiting for someone to ask me to dance. I turned to Shannon again. "How about it?" I yelled, pointing at the dance floor.

She shrugged. "Why not?" And so, the two of us took those first, courageous steps into the middle of the floor. (Hey, I'm a born leader. What can I say?)

For about two seconds, I felt aware of the fact that everyone was watching us. Then I forgot about that, just as I had a few nights ago, and let myself feel the beat. Soon I wasn't thinking about anything.

"I knew we'd have a great time together!" Shannon yelled.

"Me too!" I shouted back.

Earlier that evening, just as I'd stepped out of my predance shower, the phone had rung. "Kristy!" Watson had yelled from downstairs. "It's for you."

I picked up the extension. "Hello?" I asked.

"Hey, it's Shannon. I have some bad news and good news. Which do you want first?"

"Bad news, I guess," I said. "What's up?"

"My date's temperature," she answered. "He has a fever. And chills. His mom just called and said he has the flu."

"That *is* bad news," I said.

"Yeah, but here's the good news. Now you and I can go together!"

"Cool," I said. I didn't mind going to the dance dateless, but it's always nice to have a friend to arrive with.

So that's how Shannon and I ended up dancing together and having a terrific time. I couldn't believe how happy she looked. I hadn't seen her so relaxed in a long, long time.

Anyway, my plan worked just as well as it had the other night. By the time the song was half over, the dance floor was filled with kids — and after that, it was never empty again.

After that first dance, Shannon and I strolled around for awhile to see what our friends were up to. We had to shout to make ourselves heard over the music as we gossiped about everyone at the dance.

"Claudia looks happy," said Shannon, pointing out a laughing Claud (dressed in a rented tux that looked outstanding on her) dancing with five seventh-grade boys at once. It's funny; Claudia was excited about going to a dance with her eighth-grade friends, but she ended up hanging out more with her seventh-grade friends. I was secretly glad to see that she didn't dance with Mark all night. He spent most of the evening hanging out with a bunch of guys near the refreshment table. On the other hand, Claudia's friend Josh paid plenty of attention to her.

"I think Claudia is kind of like a queen to those seventh-grade boys," I hollered to Shannon.

"Never underestimate the power of an older woman!" she yelled back, laughing. "And check out Mary Anne and Logan. They seem to be having a good time together."

I nodded. "Logan even talked her into dancing," I observed.

"Look at Cokie Mason. She looks like an ad for Jungle World," said Shannon, eyeing her carefully.

I cracked up. You'd have to have seen Cokie's outfit to believe it. She was dressed entirely in animal prints, from her dalmatian go-go boots to her leopard-skin miniskirt to her zebra top. All fake furs, of course. I noticed a couple of boys from Kelsey Middle School following her around. "I guess those Kelsey guys don't know that C-O-K-I-E spells trouble," I yelled to Shannon. "That's the problem with being from another school."

"Speaking of Kelsey boys, check out those two cute sixth-graders Jessi and Mal are with," said Shannon.

I looked. She was right — they were cute. One was an excellent dancer. He and Jessi made a striking pair. The other one was grinning at Mal.

"I think Alan's met his match too," I yelled, pointing to Alan Gray, who was dancing with a girl I didn't recognize. "Do you know her?" I asked Shannon.

She nodded, cracking up. "She goes to SDS," she said. "Her name's Sophie, and she's always pulling practical jokes and causing trouble."

"She seems like the female equivalent of Alan," I said, watching them as they started a conga line that demanded ridiculous dance steps. Then they made fun of other dancers behind their backs and had contests to see which one could catch a cookie — with no hands (I'll leave the details to your imagination). Talk about soul mates. "Personally, I'm happy for Alan," I told Shannon. "Mainly because he's out of *my* hair."

Next, Shannon pointed out that Stacey had

caught the eye of a boy from SDS. He kept bringing her glasses of punch. She'd have floated away if she'd drunk it all. "Look," I said to Shannon, nudging her as I spied Stacey hiding a glass behind the bleachers. We both laughed.

And Abby? "Nobody ever said Abby doesn't know how to have a good time," said Shannon, pointing out our newest BSC member, who danced all night to every song. She danced with boys from every one of the schools. She danced with friends. She even danced by herself — and had a great time doing it.

"Even our chaperones are having fun," I said, nodding toward the dance floor where Watson and my mom were jitterbugging.

"And look who's getting romantic," I pointed out. By then a slow number had started, and Mr. and Mrs. Kilbourne were dancing with their arms around each other. I saw Shannon smile at them.

"I think my family's going to be a lot closer from now on," Shannon confided to me. "And Tiffany and Maria are going to be happier. I'll make sure of that."

I had a feeling Shannon would be happier too. Cutting back on activities and spending more time with her sisters was going to do more than just end the Sister War.

Shannon and I had a great time that night,

between dancing and people watching. But my favorite part of the dance came near the end. That's when the DJ put on that song "I Feel Like Dancing." I looked around and caught the eye of each of the other BSC members. "Come on, guys!" I shouted, waving my arms to motion them onto the floor. Then we formed a circle and, with our hands on each other's shoulders, danced together as a club. I smiled around at my friends, and they all grinned back. That's my club. The BSC, together forever.

Dear Reader,

The idea for *Kristy and the Sister War* came first as a title — we liked the title so much that we decided to write a story to match! Kids often ask me where I get the ideas for my books and the answer is that they come from many different sources. Sometimes an idea is sparked by watching the news or reading the paper or a magazine. I read lots of magazines, everything from *The New Yorker* to *People*. The idea for BSC #84, *Dawn and the School Spirit War*, came from an article I read in a magazine.

Kids frequently send me plot ideas in their letters. I don't use those specific ideas, but the letters are still helpful, because by reading them, I find out what issues are of concern to kids, or simply what they would like to read about in future BSC books. This was how the idea for BSC #93, *Mary Anne and the Memory Garden*, came about. Lots of books have been based on things that actually happened to me or to people I know. Some baby-sitting episodes are about things that happened to me when I was a sitter. My own baby-sitting memories gave me the idea for BSC #2, *Claudia and the Phantom Phone Calls*. For me, the best story ideas come from real life. This is why when kids ask for writing tips, I always recommend that they keep a journal — not so much for writing practice, but as a source of ideas.

Happy writing,

Ann M. Martin

L. GODWIN

Ann M. Martin

About the Author

ANN MATTHEWS MARTIN was born on August 12, 1955. She grew up in Princeton, NJ, with her parents and her younger sister, Jane.

Although Ann used to be a teacher and then an editor of children's books, she's now a full-time writer. She gets the ideas for her books from many different places. Some are based on personal experiences. Others are based on childhood memories and feelings. Many are written about contemporary problems or events.

All of Ann's characters, even the members of the Baby-sitters Club, are made up. (So is Stoneybrook.) But many of her characters are based on real people. Sometimes Ann names her characters after people she knows; other times she chooses names she likes.

In addition to the Baby-sitters Club books, Ann Martin has written many other books for children. Her favorite is *Ten Kids, No Pets* because she loves big families and she loves animals. Her favorite Baby-sitters Club book is *Kristy's Big Day*. (By the way, Kristy is her favorite baby-sitter!)

Ann M. Martin now lives in New York with her cats, Gussie and Woody. Her hobbies are reading, sewing, and needlework — especially making clothes for children.

Notebook Pages

This Baby-sitters Club book belongs to _____.

I am _____ years old and in the _____

grade.

The name of my school is _____.

I got this BSC book from _____.

I started reading it on _____ and

finished reading it on _____.

The place where I read most of this book is _____.

My favorite part was when _____.

If I could change anything in the story, it might be the part when

_____.

My favorite character in the Baby-sitters Club is _____.

The BSC member I am most like is _____

because _____.

If I could write a Baby-sitters Club book it would be about __

_____.

#112 Kristy and the Sister War

In *Kristy and the Sister War*, Kristy is caught in the middle of a feud between Shannon and her sisters. When Kristy and Shannon first met, Kristy thought Shannon was a snob. Now they're friends. I think Shannon is _____ _____. Shannon participates in many school activities. Some of my activities are _____ _____. My favorite is

_____.

My least favorite is _____.
Tiffany and Maria are upset when Shannon doesn't have time to spend with them. So they start a sister war, playing all kinds of pranks on Shannon. If I were Tiffany and Maria, I would have

_____.

In the end, Shannon plans to spend more time with her sisters. I would like to spend more time with _____ _____. If we had more time together, this is what we would do: _____

_____.

KRISTY'S

Playing softball with some of my favorite sitting charges.

A gab-fest

Me, age 3. Already on the go.

SCRAPBOOK

My family keeps growing!

with Mary Anne!

David Michael, me, and Louie — the best dog ever.

Illustrations by Angelo Tillery

Read all the books
about **Kristy**
in the Baby-sitters Club series
by Ann M. Martin

Look for #113

CLAUDIA MAKES UP HER MIND

I could picture the expression on Stacey's face. She would absolutely faint with joy. I imagined myself making an announcement at a BSC meeting.

I'd be back in eighth grade.

Back where I belong.

That thought lasted about a nanosecond.

Then I thought of Mark. And Jeannie. And Shira and Joanna and Josh. And my teachers.

And my Queenship.

Was I crazy? I was going to leave my first serious boyfriend? Turn my back on four fantastic friends? Give up the first classes that didn't make me feel like a total doofus? Not to mention tossing aside the throne.

"Do I have to decide now?" I asked.

Mrs. Amer smiled. "Of course not. But I

don't want this to drag out too long. The marking period ends soon. Why don't we make an appointment — you, me, and your parents — for sometime next week?"

"Okay, fine." I said. "I'll tell them to call you."

"I know this isn't going to be an easy decision," Mrs. Amer said, standing up. "But in the long run, it'll work out. Please don't hesitate to come see me between now and then. I'm here to help."

I stood up too. "Thanks, Mrs. Amer."

We shook hands and I left.

I was kind of hoping one or two of my friends might have stayed. But the hallway was empty.

I needed to talk to someone — but who? Stacey? Mark? Jeannie?

A seventh-grade friend? An eighth-grade friend? My family? Nobody?

How could I possibly decide something like this?

Collect them all!

More titles... ▶

❏ MG22873-0	#89	Kristy and the Dirty Diapers	$3.50
❏ MG22874-9	#90	Welcome to the BSC, Abby	$3.99
❏ MG22875-1	#91	Claudia and the First Thanksgiving	$3.50
❏ MG22876-5	#92	Mallory's Christmas Wish	$3.50
❏ MG22877-3	#93	Mary Anne and the Memory Garden	$3.99
❏ MG22878-1	#94	Stacey McGill, Super Sitter	$3.99
❏ MG22879-X	#95	Kristy + Bart = ?	$3.99
❏ MG22880-3	#96	Abby's Lucky Thirteen	$3.99
❏ MG22881-1	#97	Claudia and the World's Cutest Baby	$3.99
❏ MG22882-X	#98	Dawn and Too Many Sitters	$3.99
❏ MG69205-4	#99	Stacey's Broken Heart	$3.99
❏ MG69206-2	#100	Kristy's Worst Idea	$3.99
❏ MG69207-0	#101	Claudia Kishi, Middle School Dropout	$3.99
❏ MG69208-9	#102	Mary Anne and the Little Princess	$3.99
❏ MG69209-7	#103	Happy Holidays, Jessi	$3.99
❏ MG69210-0	#104	Abby's Twin	$3.99
❏ MG69211-9	#105	Stacey the Math Whiz	$3.99
❏ MG69212-7	#106	Claudia, Queen of the Seventh Grade	$3.99
❏ MG69213-5	#107	Mind Your Own Business, Kristy!	$3.99
❏ MG69214-3	#108	Don't Give Up, Mallory	$3.99
❏ MG69215-1	#109	Mary Anne to the Rescue	$3.99
❏ MG05988-2	#110	Abby the Bad Sport	$3.99
❏ MG05989-0	#111	Stacey's Secret Friend	$3.99
❏ MG05990-4	#112	Kristy and the Sister War	$3.99
❏ MG45575-3		Logan's Story Special Edition Readers' Request	$3.25
❏ MG47118-X		Logan Bruno, Boy Baby-sitter	
		Special Edition Readers' Request	$3.50
❏ MG47756-0		Shannon's Story Special Edition	$3.50
❏ MG47686-6		The Baby-sitters Club Guide to Baby-sitting	$3.25
❏ MG47314-X		The Baby-sitters Club Trivia and Puzzle Fun Book	$2.50
❏ MG48400-1		BSC Portrait Collection: Claudia's Book	$3.50
❏ MG22864-1		BSC Portrait Collection: Dawn's Book	$3.50
❏ MG69181-3		BSC Portrait Collection: Kristy's Book	$3.99
❏ MG22865-X		BSC Portrait Collection: Mary Anne's Book	$3.99
❏ MG48399-4		BSC Portrait Collection: Stacey's Book	$3.50
❏ MG69182-1		BSC Portrait Collection: Abby's Book	$3.99
❏ MG92713-2		The Complete Guide to The Baby-sitters Club	$4.95
❏ MG47151-1		The Baby-sitters Club Chain Letter	$14.95
❏ MG48295-5		The Baby-sitters Club Secret Santa	$14.95
❏ MG45074-3		The Baby-sitters Club Notebook	$2.50
❏ MG44783-1		The Baby-sitters Club Postcard Book	$4.95

Available wherever you buy books...or use this order form.
Scholastic Inc., P.O. Box 7502, Jefferson City, MO 65102

Please send me the books I have checked above. I am enclosing $_____
(please add $2.00 to cover shipping and handling). Send check or money order–
no cash or C.O.D.s please.

Name_____ Birthdate_____

Address_____

City_____ State/Zip_____

Please allow four to six weeks for delivery. Offer good in the U.S. only. Sorry,
mail orders are not available to residents of Canada. Prices subject to change.

BSC5962

THE BABY-SITTERS CLUB®

by Ann M. Martin

Collect and read these exciting BSC Super Specials, Mysteries, and Super Mysteries along with your favorite Baby-sitters Club books!

BSC Super Specials

BSC Mysteries

More titles ➡

The Baby-sitters Club books continued...

❑ BAI47050-7	#12 Dawn and the Surfer Ghost	$3.50
❑ BAI47051-5	#13 Mary Anne and the Library Mystery	$3.50
❑ BAI47052-3	#14 Stacey and the Mystery at the Mall	$3.50
❑ BAI47053-1	#15 Kristy and the Vampires	$3.50
❑ BAI47054-X	#16 Claudia and the Clue in the Photograph	$3.99
❑ BAI48232-7	#17 Dawn and the Halloween Mystery	$3.50
❑ BAI48233-5	#18 Stacey and the Mystery at the Empty House	$3.50
❑ BAI48234-3	#19 Kristy and the Missing Fortune	$3.50
❑ BAI48309-9	#20 Mary Anne and the Zoo Mystery	$3.50
❑ BAI48310-2	#21 Claudia and the Recipe for Danger	$3.50
❑ BAI22866-8	#22 Stacey and the Haunted Masquerade	$3.50
❑ BAI22867-6	#23 Abby and the Secret Society	$3.99
❑ BAI22868-4	#24 Mary Anne and the Silent Witness	$3.99
❑ BAI22869-2	#25 Kristy and the Middle School Vandal	$3.99
❑ BAI22870-6	#26 Dawn Schafer, Undercover Baby-sitter	$3.99
❑ BA69175-9	#27 Claudia and the Lighthouse Mystery	$3.99
❑ BA69176-7	#28 Abby and the Mystery Baby	$3.99
❑ BA69177-5	#29 Stacey and the Fashion Victim	$3.99
❑ BA69178-3	#30 Kristy and the Mystery Train	$3.99
❑ BA69179-1	#31 Mary Anne and the Music Box Secret	$3.99
❑ BA05972-6	#32 Claudia and the Mystery in the Painting	$3.99

BSC Super Mysteries

❑ BAI48311-0	The Baby-sitters' Haunted House Super Mystery #1	$3.99
❑ BAI22871-4	Baby-sitters Beware Super Mystery #2	$3.99
❑ BAI69180-5	Baby-sitters' Fright Night Super Mystery #3	$4.50

Available wherever you buy books...or use this order form.
Scholastic Inc., P.O. Box 7502, Jefferson City, MO 65102-7502

Please send me the books I have checked above. I am enclosing $ _____
(please add $2.00 to cover shipping and handling). Send check or money order
— no cash or C.O.D.s please.

Name_____Birthdate_____

Address _____

City_____State/Zip_____

Please allow four to six weeks for delivery. Offer good in the U.S. only. Sorry, mail orders are not available to residents of Canada. Prices subject to change.